LOSING

D1150611

A cosmic hiccup in Elizabethan England...

Once Mel was just an ordinary teenager. Now she's a time-travelling angel! The Agency is sending her and her two angel mates, Lola and Reuben, on an assignment to sixteenth-century London, where they must rescue a troublesome teenage trio. But what, exactly, is so special about Cat, Nick and Chance? Mel can't help wondering if they're really worth all this heavenly attention.

Then disaster strikes, and there's no time for questions! Mel and her friends have to act FAST...

ANGELS UNLIMITED: LOSING THE PLOT

Annie Dalton

First published in 2001
by HarperCollins Children's Books
an imprint of HarperCollins Publishers
Ltd
This Large Print edition published by
BBC Audiobooks Ltd
by arrangement with
HarperCollins Children's Books
2005

ISBN 1 4056 6047 3

British Library Cataloguing in Publication Data

Printed and bound in Great Britain by
Antony Rowe Ltd., Chippenham, Wiltshire

CHAPTER ONE

Try to forget I'm an angel for a minute, and put yourself in my shoes.

Once upon a time, not so long ago, I lived on Earth like you. I attended your standard hell-hole comprehensive, where I spent most of my time hanging out with my mates, nattering about boys and clothes, and waiting for my real life to begin.

Don't get me wrong. I wasn't your actual, tattooed-in-rude-places bad girl. But I don't think even my best mates would have voted me Girl Most Likely to Become an Angel! My teacher, Miss Rowntree, thought I was a waste of space. 'An airhead with attitude,' she called me.

You know how it is. If enough people tell you you're dim, you start to believe it, don't you? So when I found myself at the Angel Academy, I automatically assumed there'd been some big celestial screw-up. Clearly they'd confused me with some genuinely deserving kid.

Only they hadn't.

Believe it or not, I turned out to have a natural gift for angel work.

I'm not saying I'm this like, angel genius or anything. I made some really stupid mistakes when I first got here. But the great thing about the Angel Academy is they expect you to get down to the nitty gritty stuff right away. Unlike on Earth, where you have to wait till you're practically grown up before you're allowed to do anything interesting.

To my amazement I passed my exams with flying colours. And at the end of last term, I finally got my true angel name (it's Helix if you're interested). As for my new home, well. Picture your dream holiday destination and times it by a zillion, and even that doesn't begin to do this place justice.

Sounds like I've got it made, I know. Here I am, literally living in Paradise, doing something I'm actually good at. For the first time, I'm part of something. And to top it all, this very morning, my first ever angel ID had arrived in the post.

I should have been the happiest person alive. But I wasn't. Alive that is, or happy. Because I knew that somewhere in a tiny council flat, in a distant galaxy far away, my mum was crying herself to sleep, totally convinced her eldest daughter had been tragically snuffed out, like some little candle flame. When all the time I was safe and sound on what my Great Nan likes to call The Other Side.

I know what you're thinking. What kind of loser feels unhappy in Heaven? My mates were thinking exactly the same thing. In fact, they had a real go at me.

'You never come out with us any more, Mel,' Lola complained. 'You're practically a hermit these days.'

'I'll come next time, I swear,' I mumbled guiltily. 'It's just that I volunteered to do Angel Watch tonight.'

'Yeah, right,' said Reuben. 'That's what you said last time, and the time before, and the time before that.'

'You've got to come, Boo. Today's

your big day!' Lola wailed. 'You finally got your ID!'

'Yeah, you're a bona fide trainee angel,' Reuben coaxed. 'So let's go downtown and party like we planned.'

I shook my head. 'I told you, I can't.'

Lola glowered at me. 'I thought we were your mates, Mel Beeby. But it's like you're deliberately avoiding us. How can we help you if you won't tell us what's wrong?'

It probably doesn't seem that way, but Lola Sanchez is my soul mate. The moment I set eyes on her I felt as if we'd known each other for ever, and she felt just the same way. Before she died, Lola lived in the twenty-second century, in some tough third-world city. And sometimes you can totally tell!

Reuben's the complete opposite. (Lola's nickname for him is Sweetpea.) Quarrels actually make him feel ill. But don't get the wrong idea. Reuben's no light-weight. He does martial arts, so he's got serious muscles. But unlike me and Lola, Reuben actually started life as an angel. He's only ever lived in the Heavenly City and finds humans

4

totally baffling.

Usually, the three of us are inseparable. The Three Cosmic Musketeers, Lola calls us. We're all doing Earth History for our special subject. That probably sounds like we're always memorising dates and reading history books, right? Wrong!

OK, we have to do a bit of studying, but we also make actual field trips to like, different eras in Earth's history. And like Lola says, the sheer buzz of time-travelling totally makes up for the other stuff.

But lately, I couldn't seem to muster any enthusiasm for anything. I was much too homesick. For days now, I'd been completely churned up about my family. It wouldn't have been so bad if I could let them know I was OK. But this was out of the question. Which is why I tried to take my mind off things by doing something practical, like Angel Watch.

It was getting on for midnight as I hurried across the city, and stars glittered over the skyscrapers like huge diamante brooches. I could hear the soft swoosh of traffic, and another sound—a sweet steady throbbing like a cosmic humming top. Once I'd asked Reuben where this mysterious music was coming from.

'Everything!' he said calmly.

I still don't understand how it works. I only know it's the loveliest sound I've ever heard. It's the first thing I heard after a joyrider accidentally booted me out of the twenty-first century and into the Angel Academy. These days I mostly notice it as I'm drifting off to sleep, or when I'm alone with my thoughts.

I was heading for the Agency building, way the other side of town. The Agency is the administrative hub of the entire cosmos. In other words, Angel HQ. We're generally referred to as 'cosmic agents' these days, rather than angels. This has the advantage of sounding dead crisp and professional, not to mention totally up to the minute.

The Agency is based in this futuristic glass tower. Its upper storeys literally disappear into the clouds. Gorgeous colours wash over it in waves. Every few seconds there's a burst of light overhead as celestial agents arrive or depart. Because of all the high-level cosmic activity going on inside, the tower gives off amazing vibes. I get tingles while I'm still like, *streets* away.

On this particular night, I went in through the revolving doors, tiptoed across the marble foyer, and flashed my new ID casually at the guy on the desk. Then I stepped into a lift and went humming up into the sky.

The Angel Watch centre takes up an entire floor of the Agency building. It's a massive open-plan area with hundreds of work stations. The minute you walk in, you hear a vast murmuring sound, like an invisible tide washing in and out. I was totally blown away when I realised what I was hearing. Human thoughts. Wave after wave of them. Sad, happy, funny, lonely, please-please-help-me thoughts. And thanks to the Agency, every single one is heard. They're extremely proud of this heavenly aftercare service. Though when I was living on Planet Earth, I personally had NO idea this scheme was available.

One of the night staff handed me a list. 'Here again, Mel!' she joked.

'I like coming here,' I said defensively.

It was true. It made me feel slightly less guilty about my cushy new life. Plus I got a genuine buzz out of helping people. Assuming I was helping them, of course.

I spotted a free booth next to Kwan Yin, this v. serene girl from the Academy. As I passed, I caught a glimpse of her screen.

It was horrifying. Kids, so coated in dust they looked grey, were picking through rags and Coke cans on some vast rubbish tip. One of them was about the same age as my little sister, Jade.

'Omigosh,' I said in dismay. 'What can anyone ever do to help them?'

'This,' said Kwan Yin calmly and went on beaming angelic vibes.

Once I was in my booth, I adjusted my swivel chair, and kicked off my shoes. Then I consulted my list and tapped in the access code for someone called Jordan Scarlatti.

A tiny bald baby flashed up on my screen.

New-borns often find Earth a shock to their systems, so the Agency surrounds them with homey angel vibes while they adjust. It's like goldfish. You don't dump them in chilly tap water right off, do you? You acclimatise them gradually.

Baby Jordan was in an incubator, wired up to this beeping hi-tech machine. His mum sat holding his teeny doll-sized hand through the hole in the incubator. I think she was the one who'd called us for help.

'OK, let's see what we can do,' I whispered.

Using Angel Link is totally second nature to me now. It's a kind of heavenly internet, only you don't need a machine to access help or info, just pure concentration.

First I mentally linked up to every angel in existence. And once I felt those familiar vibes whoosh through me, I transmitted them to Jordan for all I was worth.

When I'd finished, I couldn't resist plonking an angel kiss right on Jordan's button nose. Sometimes we breathe on the back of their necks or their bare tummies, a kind of angel tickle. Babies adore angelic vibes, and Jordan's baby thoughts instantly went haywire. 'Mum, Mum, an angel kissed me!'

'Ssh, it's our secret,' I said softly.

A ripple of laughter went round the centre. The other night workers were pointing at something above my head, so naturally I looked up too.

A crowd of party balloons was floating towards me. Suddenly one gave a loud POP! Sparkly streamers fell out and draped themselves around my head, making me feel a real wally.

'Surprise, surprise!' sang a familiar voice. And Lola and Reuben burst in, clutching cartons from our favourite Chinese takeaway.

As I'm sure you guessed, trainee angels are not encouraged to smuggle Shanghai noodles and crispy seaweed into the Agency building. Not to mention balloons, and heavenly party poppers.

'Are you off your heads?' I wailed, when I could get the words out.

'It's your fault, Boo,' said Lola cheerfully. 'Since you wouldn't come to the party, we had to bring the party to you!'

She dumped her stylish takeaway cartons on my desk and started peeling off tinfoil lids. Delicious smells filled the air. 'I don't know about you guys, but I'm starving,' she announced.

But at that moment, I noticed Reuben staring past her with an appalled expression. I followed his gaze. Omigosh, I thought. We are SO in trouble.

Lola saw my face and spun round in alarm.

Standing behind her was our headmaster.

CHAPTER TWO

Let me explain that Michael is not, repeat NOT, your typical headmaster.

As well as running our school, he's a v. big cheese at the Agency. He's also an archangel. Plus he totally doesn't take care of himself. On this particular night, he wore a beautiful suit which already looked as if he'd slept in it.

Rather surprisingly, he didn't mention the balloons or the takeaway, just said, 'Here again, Melanie? That's three times this week.'

Michael has this terrifying ability to see into your soul, which I completely didn't need.

'I LIKE doing Angel Watch,' I said. 'Is that so hard to believe?'

'Not at all.' Michael dragged a chair into my overcrowded little booth, which smelled suspiciously like a tiny Chinese restaurant.

'Oh, Jordan's looking much better,' he beamed. 'I'll just check his light levels.' He touched a key with a fancy L on it (which I'd totally never noticed) and the incubator filled with golden sparkles.

'Wow!' I breathed. 'How did you do that?'

Michael laughed. 'I didn't! *You* did.'

But I couldn't really take it in. I could feel Lola and Reuben silently panicking behind me. Should they whisk our Chinese goodies out from under Michael's nose? Or act like it was nothing to do with them and hope he didn't ask awkward questions?

To my amazement, Michael solved the problem by helping himself to a spring roll. 'Did you get these from The Silver Lychee?' he asked.

Lola gave a cautious nod.

'Thought so,' he mumbled happily. 'The chef's a genius.'

Sitting next to an archangel is an experience. Seeing one sploshing on the soy sauce is something else. Suddenly Lola cracked and reached for a spring roll. Soon we were all tucking in.

Michael took off his gorgeous jacket

and hung it over his chair. 'Who's next on your list, Melanie?'

Light levels really soar when there's an archangel in the vicinity, so we whizzed through my list with no effort whatsoever.

'That about wraps it up,' I said at last. 'Thanks for your help.'

I was expecting Michael to put on his jacket and go back to his office. But he said, 'Erm, how's the time-travel going, Melanie?'

'It's OK,' I sighed.

But it's impossible to lie to an archangel, so after a few seconds I came clean. 'I can't really see the point,' I admitted. 'All that hanging around being immortal and invisible. I thought we'd at least get to materialise. But Mr Allbright said very few angels develop the ability.'

I'd felt unbelievably depressed when Mr A told us this. I was like, 'Then why bother?'

'Your teacher's right.' Michael's eyes twinkled. 'Though agents have been known to make a fluke appearance in an emergency!'

14

'Oh ha ha,' I said. You see, on my first ever time-trip, I got a teeny bit carried away. I materialised without Agency permission, and almost got myself expelled.

By this time I was starting to wonder what was going on. We'd finished the takeaway ages ago, but Michael showed no sign of wanting to break up the party. Plus he kept doing that church steeple thing with his fingers, as if he was working up to asking us something.

'I'm sorry you're having doubts, Mel,' he said at last. 'You see, we've got this, er—situation on Earth. I'd been hoping you three could help out.'

Something inside me instantly sprang to attention. When archangels ask for help, it's got to be major.

'What kind of situation?' Reuben asked.

'It's actually more of a glitch. But if it isn't caught—' Michael corrected himself hastily. 'I mean, *monitored*, it could be dangerous. Perhaps even catastrophic.'

Words like these are music to Lola's

twenty-second-century ears.

'You said the three of us,' she said eagerly. 'You mean we'd be going by ourselves?'

'You do work exceptionally well as a team. But if Melanie's lost interest—'

'She hasn't. Have you, Boo?' Lola interrupted.

'I haven't?' I said.

'No way,' said Reuben firmly.

Michael cleared his throat. 'I should warn you this is one of the more volatile eras in Earth's history. A time of love, hate, treachery.'

'Sounds like fun,' grinned Lola.

'So when is this glitch exactly?' asked Reuben.

'It's not an actual glitch yet,' said Michael confusingly. 'More of a *potential* glitch. If it does appear, it will probably show up in Elizabethan London, around 1579, say.'

'So this is like, a research trip, not an actual mission, right?' I was pretty sure the Agency didn't send new trainees on solo missions.

'That's right,' Michael agreed, just a shade too quickly. 'Technically speaking, it's not a mission as such. As I said, it's a delicate situation.'

I was puzzled. Usually Michael is the most straightforward being in the universe. But tonight, it was like everything he said had this weird double meaning.

'I don't get it,' I said. 'Are you saying we can do stuff, so long as we do it like, unofficially?'

Our headmaster began to construct a new steeple with his fingers. 'Just remember that you didn't hear it from me,' he said very quietly.

I stared at him in bewilderment. What kind of an answer was that?

'Erm,' said Lola, 'What if we don't find your glitch?'

Michael suddenly looked weary. 'I can't really go into details at this stage.'

'Can't or won't?' I said cheekily.

Michael's expression was cagey. 'All you need to know is that if it isn't checked, it will leave the way wide open to the Opposition.'

I still feel queasy when I hear that word. I was totally shocked when I found out there were evil forces which

17

wage war on angels for like, fun. The Agency refers to these forces as the Opposition. My mates and I call them PODS, as in Powers of Darkness.

Unlike us, they have no actual shape of their own. But over the centuries they've developed a scary ability to take on any shape they like.

On my first time-trip to Earth, I tangled with a PODS agent who was the image of a boy I fancied at my old school. This boy (the human one) was gorgeous, but really bad news, so for obvious reasons, I'd kept this humiliating crush to myself. Yet somehow the PODS Agency had all this deeply personal info about me. It made me hot and bothered just thinking about it.

I realised Lola was talking to me. 'Mel, are you OK?'

'Er, yeah,' I said. 'When do we go?'

'As I was saying, now would be best,' said Michael.

'Oh, wha-at? Can't we at least go home to change?'

I have these perfect trouble-shooting outfits in my wardrobe, but nine times out of ten, I have to charge off in what I happen to be wearing at the time, which is usually something v. short and sparkly. Just what you need, when you're off to do battle with the Powers of Darkness.

'All right,' Michael sighed. He ruffled my hair affectionately and I felt about a zillion angel volts sizzle through me. 'But be quick.'

And with archangel fingerprints tingling all over my scalp, I said hoarsely, 'I will.'

'Do you guys get the feeling this mission could be really big?' Reuben said, as we hurried back to school.

'Really vague, more like,' I grumbled. 'I mean, first it's a situation. Then it's a glitch. Ooh, then it's only a *potential* glitch. And we're not on a mission, we're just taking a look. Erm, no, scrub that! I should have said *unofficially* taking a look!'

'It has to be vague, Mel, you know that,' said Reuben. 'Humans have free will. You can't say what's *going* to happen. Just what *might* happen.'

'Oh, honestly! Will you just listen to

yourself?' I complained.

'Hey, what's your problem?' said Lola.

I took a deep breath. 'We're supposed to be divine messengers, or whatever. Only we never actually materialise, so most humans never get the message! Duh! So can someone please tell me what we're FOR!'

My friends stared at me in surprise. I was quite surprised myself. Michael was right. I did have doubts, loads of them. Now they'd all come splurting out at once.

'I just want to know what we're for,' I repeated in a quieter voice. 'Like, if humans have this free will everyone goes on about, how come we're allowed to influence them, anyway?'

'You said it,' said Reuben. 'We *influence* them. Beam vibes, help them remember who they are. We don't make them do stuff.'

'Totally,' agreed Lola. 'The PODS put on enough pressure as it is.'

Reuben grinned. 'If it helps, just think of angels as alarm clocks.'

I couldn't help laughing. 'As what?'

His eyes glinted. 'We wake humans up!'

Lola put her arm round me. 'Come on, Boo. You should be wildly excited. Can you believe they're letting us do a solo trip?'

'Yeah, this sounds more up Orlando's street,' Reuben agreed.

Orlando is one of our seniors. Not only is he an angel genius, he's heart-meltingly gorgeous. But he's so into his studies, he genuinely doesn't notice the effect he has on girls.

Lola gave me a sly nudge. 'Melanie wishes Orlando was coming too.'

'I do not,' I said huffily.

'He's probably off on some hush-hush Agency project,' said Reuben.

'They didn't pick us because Orlando's unavailable, you know,' I objected. 'They picked us because we're good.'

'Oooh!' teased Lola. 'Someone's feeling better!'

I was, actually. 'Hey,' I said suddenly. 'Do you think angels are wired so they like, *need* to do angel work?'

My friends exchanged weary glances, zipped their lips and threw away invisible keys.

'OK, OK, I'll read the boring cosmic manual!' I sighed. 'Now can we just drop it?'

Back at the school dorm, I put on my new T-shirt, a pair of low-slung Triple 5 Soul jeans and big funky boots. I swapped a couple of hoop earrings for business-like little studs. Then I threw a few girly necessities into my rucksack, grabbed my jacket and I was ready to go.

I checked out of the window and saw an Agency limo already waiting, its lights blinking in the dark. Lola tapped on my door. We're such close friends, we're practically twins. And our taste in clothes is so similar, it's spooky. Except that being from the future, my soul-mate always looks that bit more outrageous!

Tonight, she had on the coolest sunglasses, with misty blue lenses. One lens had a tiny diamante star in the corner. 'You look great!' I told her.

The limo dropped us back at HQ,

then we hurtled down to Departures. Michael looked pointedly at his watch.

'We aren't *that* late,' I panted.

Lola grinned. 'Plus, like you always say, Time doesn't actually exist.'

Michael hustled us along corridors, giving us a last-minute briefing as we went. 'You'll be splitting up, I'm afraid. Each of you has been allocated—' he coughed. 'I mean, will be monitoring a different human.'

'So much for the research trip,' I mouthed at Lola.

'I *think* I'm right in saying it's not a plague year,' Michael was saying.

Workers in white fluorescent suits were giving our portal a last-minute service. The chief maintenance guy gave us a bashful grin. On Earth, Al would be an ideal heavy, a doorman at a nightclub or something. But he's actually incredibly shy. He makes these agonizing little jokes but he totally can't look you in the eye.

Michael dished out our angel tags while we waited. We always wear them when we're on official business. They help us stay in contact with other

23

angels through the Link. Plus they're v. useful if we want to get somewhere in a hurry. Since we were going to Earth without a supervising adult, we also got issued with these really hi-tech Agency watches.

'Ready when you are, kids,' said Al, and we stepped into the portal.

Reuben was singing under his breath. I recognised the lyrics of a tune he'd been working on. *'You're not alone,'* it went, *'You're not alone,'* over and over.

'That's a cool tune, Sweetpea,' Lola said. 'Let's put a little harmony in there.' Lola has a beautiful voice. She literally sings like an angel.

I sing like a frog, basically, but I joined in just the same.

When Michael heard us singing in the time portal, he got this weird look on his face. At first I thought it was because his regular agents don't tend to sing on take-off. But he didn't look like, annoyed. He looked sort of touched and upset. He actually made a move towards us, as if he was going to say something. Then at the last minute, he checked himself and gave Al the thumbs-up.

'Remember,' he called to us, 'stay alert.'

The door slid shut.

'Yeah, the Agency needs lerts,' Lola quipped under her breath.

I waved at Michael through the glass, trying not to laugh.

'What's plague, Mel?' Reuben hissed into my ear.

I explained that the plague was one of the most terrifyingly contagious human diseases ever. I'd just reached the part about those disgusting purple boils, when our portal lit up like a fairground and we were blasted out of Heaven and into the slipstream of history.

Time-travel, Agency-style, is unbelievably speedy. Entire centuries flash past your eyes in a multi-coloured blur.

Shortly after take-off, we passed a major Opposition outpost. They're quite easy to spot, generally showing up as whirlpools of dark icky energy. The Agency only sends really top-flight trouble-shooters there. Personally, just whizzing past one gave me the chills.

Then I remembered something that Mr Allbright said. He said *nothing in the cosmos ever stays the same*. Like, a golden era can collapse in ruins and a dark one can have a major change of heart.

I remembered something else too. He said it only takes one wide-awake human to make a difference!

But as we hurtled towards our destination, we started getting a weird strobing effect. Dark light dark light dark light. Like a cosmic zebra crossing.

It looked as if we were heading for a time and place where the forces of light and darkness were totally equal. It was deeply disturbing to look at. I hastily put on my shades.

'Erm?' I said. 'Aren't fifty-fifty set-ups incredibly dangerous? Aren't they the ones which easily tip like, either way?'

But I never got my answer. With a final blinding burst of light, we were catapulted into Time. When I opened my eyes, the time-portal had vanished. So had my friends.

I was alone in Elizabethan London.

It was raining heavily. And there was no light anywhere.

CHAPTER THREE

Eventually I twigged. This was not Cosmic Darkness with a capital D, it's just that street-lights hadn't been invented yet.

'Aargh! What is that?' I clapped my hands over my nose.

Think of your local rubbish dump on a sweltering summer's day, add a spot of raw sewage and a dash of wood-smoke, and you'll get an idea of the extreme niffiness of Elizabethan London.

My Agency watch flashed, informing me I'd been on this mission for exactly thirty, oops, thirty-one seconds.

We're meant to run through this three-step procedure, as soon as we touch down. Luckily, I'd memorised this section of the manual.

'STEP ONE,' I recited. 'Adjust angel senses, if necessary. Conditions may be primitive, causing distress to divine personnel.'

Tell me about it! I hastily made the

necessary adjustments, doing my best to avoid taking in any actual oxygen. To my relief, the pong became more bearable.

I was becoming aware of low grumbling sounds. Suddenly my surroundings lit up with a lurid blue light. The lightning lasted long enough for me to see scruffy thatched roofs and timber house-fronts, all leaning every which way, and several rats scavenging in the garbage. Then I was back in darkness.

Since I became an angel, I kind of tolerate rats, but I'm not what you'd call a fan. I carried on bravely with my check-list.

'STEP TWO. Acclimatise to local thought levels . . .'

Elizabethan thought-levels turned out to be soothingly low-density. Plus, they had a bubbly feel-good vibe, which I totally wasn't expecting.

My watch let out a beep. Time for Step Three. Should be homing in on my subject any minute now.

The rain was hammering down by this time, and the flashes of lightning were v. close together.

Two men in cloaks hurried past. One held up a burning torch to light their way. It gave off a strong, vaguely familiar smell, like creosote or tar.

Roars of laughter were coming from a house with a green bush over the door. Stale beer fumes and savoury cooking smells wafted out. The door opened and someone lurched into the street, singing at the top of his voice.

This is the place, I thought. I can't explain how I knew. It's an angel thing. Like a tiny zing of angel electricity inside your heart.

I took a deep breath and went in.

Inside, yellowish candles gave out a spluttering light and a strong smell of fat.

I dutifully scanned my immediate environment, like Mr Allbright says we should, in case any other cosmic agents were passing through. They weren't, which I found quite surprising. We usually spot loads of Earth angels knocking around.

The tavern was crowded with customers, all quaffing ale and tucking into platters of stew. It was a real mix. Well-off types wearing starched ruffs and gorgeous silks and velvets, mingling cheerfully with poorer people. Though I think there must have been some law which said the poor had to wear depressing clothes, because the majority of the customers were dressed in these like, dingy dung colours.

All this candlelight was highly atmospheric, but unfortunately it didn't quite reach into the corners. I had to wander around, peering foolishly into shadows. Where oh where was my human?

One corner was filled by a huge snoring drunk. As I watched, he scratched furiously at his head. Still totally zonked, the drunk then began foraging in his armpit. Hey, fleas *and* body lice, I thought. Groovy!

In another corner, a young man was scribbling on a piece of parchment, between mouthfuls of stew. Hmmn, homesick foreigner, I decided. Possibly French. Could this be my human? He was WAY the most stylish dresser in the tavern.

I listened hopefully to my heart. Uh-uh, I decided regretfully. No zing.

A plump woman was ferrying flagons of ale between the tables, looking hot and flustered. 'Where's that girl got to?' she complained to a man in an apron. 'It's all me and Nettie can do to keep up.'

Being an angel, I understood her perfectly, but her words had an almost American twang; nothing like English speech in my day.

'Don't be hard on her, wife,' said the man calmly. ' 'Tis my brother's last night in port. He and Cat will be saying their farewells.'

ZING!

That's her, I thought. That's my human!

I made my way around the tavern, as if I was being pulled along by an invisible string, until I reached a dark winding staircase. By the time I reached the top, it wasn't a pulling sensation. It was a shout. *She's here*!

A girl's voice floated through an open door. 'Why won't you take me?'

I slipped through the door into a

little room. By modern standards it was empty. Bare floorboards, a bed, a wooden chest, a jug, and a small basin. Two stubs of candle gave a flickering light.

Cat had her back to me. She seemed to be in the middle of a big argument with a wild-haired man in seaboots. He was big and burly with an impressive collection of scars. A pearl the size of a pear-drop dangled from his ear.

'I told you before! It's no life for a little maid at sea.'

'I'm not a little maid, I'm thirteen,' Cat snapped. 'And I can do anything a man can do and more.'

She turned and I saw her properly for the first time.

She was beautiful. Even in this light, I could tell her eyes were green. But it was the colour of her skin which really took me by surprise. It was like Demerara sugar, at the exact moment it melts into caramel.

I am so dense. I had no *idea* there were any black Elizabethans.

Cat twiddled a wiry black curl which had escaped from her cap. 'Don't leave

33

me,' she pleaded. 'Living here, I feel like a freak at a fair.'

She put on a bumpkin voice. 'What shall we do tonight, Ebenezer? Oh, let's go to the Feathers and gawp at the blackamoor. 'Tis said her father is the most fearsome pirate on the Spanish Main.'

Her voice shook with unhappiness. But I'm ashamed to say I was totally thrilled. A pirate's daughter! This had to be my coolest assignment yet!

Her dad sounded upset. 'Was I wrong to bring you to England?'

'No,' she admitted. 'I was happy when I was little.' She clutched his arm. 'Take me with you. Please.'

Her father sighed. 'Not this time, my honey.' He gave her an awkward pat. 'Come, let us part as friends. It may be many months before we meet again.'

Cat fingered a string of cowrie shells around her neck. Her face had gone totally blank and her emotions were so guarded that even *I* couldn't tell what she was feeling.

'You look just like her,' her father said huskily.

34

She dropped her shells. 'I know who I look like!' she spat. 'I see myself in the glass each morning. So if you mean to leave me behind again, go! And don't bother coming back!'

The pirate's face grew dark with anger. Moving surprisingly quietly for such a bulky man, he left without a word, closing the door behind him.

Cat instantly threw herself face-down on her bed. She cried so hard, I felt the bed shaking, yet she didn't make a sound.

I sat beside her in agonized sympathy. 'Please don't,' I begged her. 'He hates leaving you. Angels know these things.'

After bawling for five minutes max, Cat sat up and gave herself a fierce shake. 'The world is full of orphans,' she said aloud. 'They manage well enough.'

She splashed water on her face from the basin, tied an apron around her waist, blew out one candle and used the other to light her way downstairs.

'Catherine Darcy, you'll be the death of me!' her aunt scolded through the

35

uproar. 'Me and Nettie's rushed off our feet. You can start by serving these fine gentlemen by the window.'

I learned a lot about Cat as I watched her serving customers, demurely dodging the hands trying to pinch her bum or sneak down her bodice, and ignoring stupid remarks about her skin colour rubbing off. She totally didn't let it touch her. Even though her life was deeply depressing, she had this queen-like dignity which I really envied.

Suddenly the door opened and two youths burst in. 'Didn't I tell you I'd make Rosalind love me?' the tallest boy was saying. He kissed his hand to the air. 'Oh, fair Rosalind, soon you will be mine!'

'You just love the chase, Nick Ducket,' grinned his friend. 'The moment she's yours, you'll moon over sweet Beatrice or lovely Helena!'

It was hard to believe they'd been out in the same rainstorm. Nick's companion looked half-drowned, while Nick himself was just fetchingly rain-sprinkled.

As well as being good-looking (he had the most gorgeous blond hair!), Nick had bags of confidence. And his clothes were sublime.

I know it's not a nice thing to say, but his mate wasn't in the same league. His boots were so old and worn that water was actually leaking out of them. And his wet hair was plastered to his scalp, emphasising his large, rather vague eyes.

Suddenly I felt my skin prickle, which is generally a sign that other angels are in the vicinity. Maybe Michael's checking up on us, I thought.

So I was completely astonished when my mates appeared. They rushed over and we had a quick hug.

'What are you doing here?' I demanded.

Reuben nodded at the boys. 'Following them.'

Nick was waving frantically to Cat. She hastily shooed them into an empty corner.

'Have pity, sweet Cat,' he wheedled. 'Chance and I haven't eaten since yesterday noon.'

She glanced around nervously. 'All right. But pay for your drinks, or my aunt will get suspicious.'

Nick threw down some coins. 'Some spiced ale, Cat, if you please!'

She rubbed her thumb across her fingers. 'And the rest, Master Ducket.'

'You do not love me,' he complained.

She gave a scornful laugh. 'Rosalind may drop at your feet like a dead pigeon the instant you fire a poem at her! I have more sense.' Flouncing her skirts, she bustled off to fetch their ale.

Nick grinned. 'I'll have to tame that little wildcat in a year or so.'

His friend didn't answer. He had an oddly misty expression. Actually, I started to wonder if maybe he wasn't quite all there.

'It's so weird that they're friends,' I said to the others. 'Why didn't the Agency say so in the first place?'

A grubby white puppy appeared from somewhere. It made an immediate beeline for Reuben, collapsing beside him in a sprawl of gangly paws, looking up adoringly.

Animals *love* pure angels. It's like hanging out with Doctor Dolittle.

Cat sneaked two huge helpings of stew to her mates while her aunt wasn't looking. 'Here's some bread to mop up the gravy,' she whispered.

'Stay, Cat,' Nick coaxed her. 'You're looking so pretty today.'

Chance started eating ravenously. 'Yes, stay, Cat,' he mumbled. 'Nick's got a proposition for you.'

Cat's eyes narrowed. 'Another one?'

Nick acted hurt. 'This will make us rich.'

'Don't tell me,' she scoffed. 'With his dying breath, an old alchemist gave you the recipe for turning lead into gold. But you're prepared to share it with me, in return for some more stew.'

Nick clutched his chest, as if she'd just stabbed him through the heart. 'So young, yet so cruel!'

Cat grinned. 'I'm young, but I didn't just fall out of the nest,' she called, as she flew off to serve new customers.

I quickly gave my mates the lowdown on Cat's unusual family history.

'Nick's amazing too,' said Lola

loyally. 'He knows Greek and Latin, plus he plays the lute. And he writes poetry.'

'And what a dish,' I sighed.

Reuben was tickling the puppy's tummy. To the customers, of course, it looked as if it was just rolling around on the ground in sheer puppy high spirits!

'What's your boy called again?' I asked politely.

He gave a deep sigh. 'Chance.'

'That's a funny name.'

'No comment,' Reuben said darkly.

Chance had really perked up now he'd eaten. Only unfortunately, he'd gone to the other extreme. When Cat joined them, he started on some involved story about how his landlord just slung him out for no reason. I've got to admit, Chance had quite a knack for storytelling. He seemed to know how to make dead ordinary things sound incredibly dramatic. But it was like no-one could get a word in!

Cat was sweet, though. 'Don't worry. We won't let you sleep on the street.'

His eyes lit up. 'It wouldn't be the

first time I've been homeless!' he said eagerly. 'Did I tell you about when I came to London? It was the middle of winter. Snow was falling—'

'I thought you arrived in May,' she objected.

'So I did,' he said promptly. 'There was an unusually late fall of snow that year. One night, I woke up in a doorway, half-dead with cold, and found myself covered in a thin layer of white, like a poor man's shroud—'

Reuben rolled his eyes. I felt sorry for him. Me and Lola both had v. cool humans to take care of. Chance was just really sad!

Unfortunately, Lola picked that moment to put the boot in. 'I've got this feeling Nick might be really famous when he grows up,' she bragged.

Reuben shuddered. 'Famous? Him? After what he was saying about cock fights, on the way here?'

She scowled. 'Animal rights haven't been invented yet, you idiot. They don't know any better.'

Suddenly I noticed several men

moving stealthily towards the Frenchman's table.

'Erm,' I said uneasily, 'I'm getting bad vibes.'

Then someone shrieked, 'The traitor has a knife!'

And next minute total chaos broke out.

CHAPTER FOUR

The Frenchman's chair was pulled from under him, sending him sprawling. Then the table went over. Ink and leftover stew flew everywhere.

Someone bellowed, 'Stand up, you Spanish dog! Fight like a man!' And someone else yanked the Frenchman to his feet.

'The knife was only to sharpen my quill, monsieurs,' he stammered.

But the men started shoving him around, trying to make him fight.

Naturally, we were doing our best to transmit helpful vibes, but it took some concentration, believe me. Luckily Cat's uncle came charging up from his cellar and calmed things down. And after a lot of extremely unpleasant name-calling, the Frenchman was allowed to leave unharmed.

Lola was horrified. 'Will someone tell me what's so wrong with Spain?' she demanded.

As it happened, the Tudors were

about the only thing I'd liked about history lessons at my old school. I think it was that irresistible combination of blood, gore and fashion! So I was able to give my mates a speedy history lesson.

'The Spanish wanted a Protestant to rule England. Sorry, I mean a Catholic,' I added hastily. 'That's right, they definitely wanted Queen Elizabeth to turn Catholic, so she could marry their king. But she said, "No way, José," so they plotted to get rid of her.'

Reuben was shocked. 'You mean like, *kill* her?'

'They tried everything!' I said knowledgeably. 'Poisoned dresses, hired assassins.'

'Poisoned dresses!' Lola was impressed.

'One time they sent warships to invade England,' I told them. 'But the English beat them off.'

Then I did a hasty calculation. 'Oh, hang on. Maybe the Spanish Armada hasn't happened yet . . . Oh, I don't know! Anyway, I'm telling you,

44

this Spanish thing dragged on for like, decades.'

Reuben looked confused. 'Mel, the guy wasn't even *Spanish*!'

Lola shrugged. 'He was foreign, wasn't he?'

I could tell the incident had put her totally on edge.

Michael warned us it would be like this, I thought. Elizabethans are SO intense. One minute everyone's having a mellow time, then suddenly, total mayhem!

I think the bad vibes had got to Chance too. Because with absolutely no warning, he jumped up and started doing acrobatics. Back-flips, cartwheels, walking on his hands.

'What on earth?' said Reuben.

Everyone was staring open-mouthed. No-one knew what to make of this lunatic.

Once he'd got everyone's attention, Chance somersaulted across the tavern at electrifying speed. Then, like a character in a musical, he jumped on a chair and started to sing. An extremely rude song to judge from the actions.

By the time he reached the last verse, the customers were laughing so much, they could hardly stand!

'Where did you learn tumbling?' Cat hissed as he took his bow.

'Oh, the gypsies taught me,' he mumbled.

Nick came bounding over to join him. After some conferring, the boys launched into a drinking song. Nick had a wonderful voice, heaps better than Chance's. When they'd finished, Chance left Nick to charm the punters with a truly beautiful ballad.

Afterwards, everyone bought them drinks, and before long everyone was getting happily smashed.

Lola was full of admiration. 'Chance totally changed the atmosphere,' she said. 'That was pure genius!'

'Pure adrenaline, you mean,' Reuben scoffed. 'It's like he *had* to do something, even if it meant making a total spectacle of himself. Have you noticed how tense he is? That kid is hiding something.'

I kind of agreed with him, actually. Something about Chance just didn't add up.

During the singsong, I'd noticed three girls chatting to Cat. What with their lurid make-up and worldly-wise expressions, it didn't exactly take a rocket scientist to figure out how they earned their living. After a bit of arguing, they called Chance over.

'Cat says you need a place to stay,' said a girl with a mole on her cheek. 'We've got a cubbyhole you could use, haven't we, Nell?'

'Tell us about yourself,' suggested Nell.

'Oh, please don't,' Reuben groaned.

But Chance was off like a wind-up rabbit, telling them how his family had fallen on hard times. Desperate to help out, he'd gone out one night to poach the squire's deer, and got caught. Luckily a mate helped him to escape from the local lock-up.

'There was nothing to do but come to London and seek my fortune. It was the month of May, but instead of blossom, snow was falling. One night I woke up in a doorway, half-dead with cold—'

'All together now,' Lola giggled.

'—and found myself covered in a thin layer of white, like a poor man's shroud,' we chorused.

But by the time Chance had finished this ridiculous yarn, the girls had agreed he could stay.

'We'll take care of your sweetheart, Cat!' they teased her, as they got up to leave.

'We're going to the playhouse tomorrow,' Nick reminded Chance. He pinched Cat's cheek. 'You come too.'

She glowered. 'You just want me to help you with your plan.'

'I'll call for you,' Nick insisted.

Reuben followed Chance and his new landladies into the night.

'Don't do anything I wouldn't do,' I called, as my soul-mate skipped off with dishy Nick.

After the last customers had stumbled home, Cat took a candle-stump and climbed up to her little attic.

I'd have fallen straight into bed, personally. But she patiently peeled off layer after layer, including a rib-crushing corset (a *corset*!), until she was only wearing her petticoat.

She washed herself thoroughly with squishy-looking home-made soap, then said her prayers. And at the end she gabbled quickly, 'Please bring my father safely home,' which I presumed meant she'd forgiven him.

Then Cat climbed into bed, snuffed out her candle, tucked her hand under her cheek, and instantly fell asleep.

Watching humans sleep is really touching. Their daytime disguises just fall away, and you see right into their souls.

Cat's dreams bore absolutely no resemblance to her daytime life. They were filled with crying gulls and the snap and billow of sails. And when she strained her eyes, she could see the shore, a blue shadow on the horizon.

But then the sun came up over the rooftops and birds began twittering outside her window. And it was time for Cat to start another day.

Nick turned up shortly after ten.

'*Omigosh*,' I sighed. 'He's even better looking by daylight!'

I noticed Lola behind him, pulling

faces. 'Hands off! This human's mine,' she teased. Strangely, she didn't sound quite as pleased about it as she had the day before.

Cat grudgingly consented to take Nick to Chance's lodgings.

'I have not agreed to anything. I want to see how he is, that's all,' she said and immediately went marching off. She had brought bread and cold meat for Chance, wrapped in a cloth.

The street was dazzlingly bright after the tavern. Lola and I put our shades on, and I hooked my arm through hers. 'So what's Golden Boy's place like?'

She rolled her eyes. 'Messy! You know boys!'

But I thought Lola sounded just a bit too perky. I don't know why, but I got the feeling she was keeping something from me.

I couldn't believe how noisy London was in these times. Wooden carts thundering over cobbles, bells pealing, plus all the street-sellers shouted practically non-stop.

Nick bought a red rose from a flower girl and stuck it in his cap.

Oh, what a poser! I thought. And I decided it was high time gorgeous Nick was dislodged from his pedestal. I gave Lola a nudge. 'Bet the flower's for that Rosalind bimbo.'

She gave me a hurt look. 'I think it looks really good on him.'

'Ooh,' I teased. 'Looks like you're carrying a bit of a torch.'

Lola glared at me. But luckily at that moment Cat and Nick got a spurt on and we had to go galloping after them.

Cat went beetling off down a maze of alleyways, until she reached a rickety tenement built of wood and thatch. Nick caught her up at the door, and started nosing in Cat's bundle while they waited for someone to let them in. She slapped his hand away.

'I see you have favourites, Cat,' he said huffily. 'Chance gets breakfast, yet I must buy my own.'

'If you're hungry, it's because you squander your father's money at cards,' she snapped. 'Chance has nobody to care for him.'

'Push the door, Cat, and walk in,' called a girl's voice.

We piled in after her into a little front room where Reuben was calmly practising martial arts knee-bends.

'You survived then,' I teased.

He grinned. 'Naturally. The girls are cool. Can you believe they've got him writing love letters to earn his keep!'

We quickly moved in to do a spot of angelic eavesdropping.

Chance was at the table in his shirt-sleeves, scribbling away. The girls clustered around him, with awed expressions.

One of the girls was mending Chance's doublet for him.

Nick pulled a sour face at Cat. 'Poor Chance has *nobody*,' he mimicked.

Chance turned to Nell. 'This is what you said. "Dearest Jem, I remember your sweet face as we walked by the river..."'

As she heard her words read back, Nell blushed to her ears. 'Tell me how to end it,' she begged.

'As quickly as possible,' Nick suggested in a sarky voice.

Chance tried to ignore him. 'Did Jem give you that half a sixpence around your neck?' She nodded. 'How about something like, "I wear your token night and day. It shines as brightly as when you first gave it to me."'

'Hurry up, man,' said Nick impatiently. 'We've got better things to do than listen to your bad poetry.'

Chance looked hurt. 'It's not supposed to be poetry. It's a letter.'

Sympathetic Nell came to his rescue. 'It's three years since I saw my Jem,' she said. 'My letter can wait.'

The other girl bit off her thread and gave Chance his doublet back. 'Farewell, Tom,' the girls called after him affectionately.

Lola and I almost banged heads in the doorway. 'Farewell who?' we said simultaneously.

Cat had gone storming out. The boys had to run to catch up with her, and so did we. She kept up her cracking pace for a few minutes. Then she glared at Chance. 'Why do you *do* that?'

He gave a baffled shrug. 'What?'

'All these lies! You even lie about your name. "My friends call me

Chance", that's what you said.'

'It's true!' he blustered.

'Really! What about that man who came for you, wasn't he looking for someone named Robert? And now you're Tom or Dick or is it Harry?'

Chance looked completely panic-stricken. He was actually cringing, like a dazed little mole being dragged into daylight.

Nick tried to interrupt but Cat was unstoppable. 'You have more names than the tavern dog! Customers call him Snowball one day and Killer the next until he—'

She stopped abruptly. Desperate to shut her up, Nick had whipped the rose out of his hatband and presented it to her with a bow.

'No more of this,' he laughed. 'For what's in a name? Would not this rose smell as sweetly, if it were called turnip or herring, or—or *hairy nostril!*'

I felt the weirdest tingle. Like I'd already heard these words, or something very like them, before. They had a similar effect on Chance, because he stopped looking like a dazzled mole, and broke into a delighted smile.

But Cat just stared at the rose. She had forgotten to close her mouth and there was the faintest flush under her golden skin.

Oh-oh, I thought. Complications! I nudged Lola. 'I think Cat fancies your Nick,' I whispered.

Reuben looked smug. 'You've only just noticed, haven't you.'

'When did you notice then?' I said sullenly.

He gave me his most seraphic smile. 'The first time I saw her.'

Suddenly Lola took off her sunglasses. I was horrified to see she was crying.

'Lollie, what is it?'

But she could hardly get the words out. 'It's Nick,' she wailed at last. Then she glowered through her tears. 'He's the bad guy, OK? Dumb old Lola got the doofus.'

'Hey, where did that come from?' I said, startled. 'This isn't a contest, you know.'

'I wouldn't say he's an out-and-out

bad guy,' said Reuben comfortingly. 'He's just a bit full of himself. It's probably hormones.'

Lola was in such a state, that she actually stamped. 'It's not his hormones. It's his *heart*, you idiot! All he thinks about is getting people to do what he wants. He's on the make, twenty-four hours a day. It's like he can't stop.'

And she told us that after Nick left the Feathers the previous evening, he'd stopped off at various shady gambling dens, ending up at some total dive where people were forcing this poor ape to ride around on a horse.

'You're kidding,' I said.

'These half-starved bulldogs were just waiting for it to fall off! And Nick watched,' she choked.

I put my arm around her. 'But that doesn't make him a bad person, Lollie. You said yourself, animal rights haven't been invented yet.'

'Boo, he was actually laughing. He thought it was funny!' Lola hid her face in her hands. 'Then we finally got back to his place, and he fell asleep and all that cruelty just melted away. And I watched him sleeping. He has such beautiful dreams,' she said earnestly. 'And it's like I saw the real him.'

I had a flash of inspiration. 'You think he's our glitch, don't you?'

'Yes. No. Oh, I don't know,' she said wretchedly.

As we watched, Nick pushed back his hair and smiled into Cat's eyes.

Lola's right, I thought. It has to be him. He's clever and gorgeous, but he's just too smooth for his own good.

Reuben beamed at Lola. 'This is great! We finally know what we're doing here.'

'Yeah! Dingaling!' I did a bad impersonation of an alarm clock. 'We have to wake up Golden Boy and save him from himself.'

I told myself this was the right, the only, decision. Chance was a real character but basically a loser. Cat was fabulous, but as an Elizabethan girl, her career prospects were painfully limited.

We're professionals, I told myself bravely. We aren't *allowed* to have favourites. And on that basis, we have to nominate talented go-getting Nick as Elizabethan Human Most Likely to Succeed.

'So that's settled,' I said. 'We'll get dishy Nick Ducket back on track and everything will be cool.'

'Phew! What a relief,' said Reuben.

And like people in a toothpaste ad, we gave each other big cheesy smiles.

CHAPTER FIVE

We were down by the docks, dangling our feet off a jetty, three angels and three humans in a row, listening to Nick pitch his latest money-making scheme. Well, Chance and Reuben were listening.

Me and Lola tuned out, the minute we realised Nick was proposing some dodgy gambling scam. I'm thick when it comes to cards and Lola was just depressed. Here we were, mad keen to help Nick become his new improved self, and he totally wouldn't co-operate.

I'm fairly sure Cat was thinking about her dad. She kept glancing wistfully at the sailing ships riding at anchor in the harbour.

I love the smell of docks: salt and tar and fresh wood shavings. Mmmn! I shut my eyes to have a good sniff, and was impressed to see gold sparkles dancing past my eyelids. 'I'm getting cosmic sparkles!' I announced excitedly.

Lola instantly shut her eyes. 'Me too! Wonder what that's about?'

'Could it be something to do with that little feel-good vibe they've got going here?' I said tentatively.

'I suppose!' Lola lifted her face to the sun, enjoying the rays.

'Maybe it's because the Elizabethan world has like totally opened up,' I suggested. 'Exciting new lands to explore. New discoveries and stuff. You can practically taste the excitement in the air.'

Especially down here, I thought dreamily, with all these beautiful ships getting ready to sail who knows where.

Lola frowned. 'I'll tell you what's weird, Boo. I mean, this has to be the vibiest time we've visited so far.'

'Totally,' I agreed.

'So, why isn't the place *stiff* with angels? I haven't seen a single cosmic agent of any description, have you?'

'Actually, no—' I began.

'Will you shut up!' Reuben grumbled. 'I'm trying to make sense of all this underworld lingo Nick's spouting. What is a "fingerer", anyway?'

Lola sighed. 'He's trying to involve Cat in a sting.'

'A what?' said Reuben.

'A hustle,' I suggested. 'A scam?'

Reuben still looked blank.

'OK,' said Lola. 'Did they tell you about gambling on your Earth Skills course?'

Reuben looked cautious. 'Kind of. Not sure I got it, though.'

'Nick wants Cat to dupe someone into thinking he's playing cards with a pair of total bozos, then he and Chance will take him for everything he's got.'

'No way. Cat will never go along with it,' Reuben said firmly. 'Will she, Mel?'

Lola sighed. 'In case you haven't noticed, Nick has this amazing way of making people do what he wants.'

'I'm talking about some law student freshly up from the country,' Nick was saying smoothly. 'If we don't empty his pockets, someone else will.'

Cat frowned. 'And if we get caught?'

'We won't,' he said impatiently. 'Besides, Chance and I are taking all the risks. You will simply be our innocent go-between.'

She chewed her lip, trying to give the impression that she was calmly weighing up various pros and cons.

Poor Cat, I thought. I completely understood what she was going through. I mean, she didn't want Nick to think she was a pushover. On the other hand, no-one wants to look like a wuss in front of their mates, do they?

Plus I think Nick giving her that rose had made Cat feel all mixed up inside. And the bottom line was that she fancied him too much to say no.

'All right. Just this once,' she agreed reluctantly.

Nick was delighted. 'That's my Cat!'

Huh! This boy is way too cocky, I fumed to myself.

'I'll buy you a new necklace out of our winnings,' he said impulsively. 'Instead of those childish shells you wear.'

Cat glowered at him. 'Just give me my share, and I'll buy my own jewellery, Nick Ducket.'

The trio set off in the general direction of London Bridge, with us angels following close behind. On the way, Reuben was fretting. 'You can't blame Chance. He's permanently broke. Also he hero-worships Nick. But Nick seems like he's quite rich. And what if his scam goes wrong? What if the others come unstuck, because of him?'

'Maybe they won't,' I suggested. 'Maybe it'll be a doddle, like Nick says, and they'll just grab the money and run.'

My mates looked shocked.

'Oh come on,' I said. 'Humans get away with dodgy stuff all the time.'

The gaming house was attached to a riverside tavern called The Fleece. It was hardly a glitzy casino, just a room with too many tables, not enough light and almost no fresh air.

Serving wenches bustled about with refreshments, but you could tell food and drink were not the point of this place. Money—winning it, losing it—that was the point. The air was jittery with anxiety.

Just inside the door, an Irishman with a silky hypnotist's voice was making three cards fly around a table like a magician.

'Keep your eyes on the Lady, my fine sirs,' he crooned. 'Don't look away, no, not for a second.'

But when the Irishman turned the cards over, the gamblers groaned with disappointment. He shook his head sorrowfully. 'Didn't I warn you to be careful?'

Reuben was beside himself. 'I just spotted a whatsisname! A sting!'

Lola burst out laughing. 'I should hope you did! No-one ever wins Find The Lady.'

Nick and Chance had been scanning the gaming house for potential victims. Now they'd clocked one, a shiny-faced law student, bragging to anyone who would listen.

At a signal from Nick, Cat moved in and went into this sexy simpleton routine.

'Two young gentlemen over there have been watching you play cards, sir,' she said in a country voice. 'And they noted your prow—prow—Oh, I dunno, 'tis a word which means "great skill".'

Loudmouth scratched his neck

64

inside its ruff. 'Prowess,' he corrected her conceitedly.

'Prowess! The very word.' Cat gave him a wide-eyed smile. 'Anyway, they sent me to inquire if you would care to play cards. They are willing to risk all the money they have with them, for the great honour of playing with such as you.' She bobbed a little curtsey.

'Then I mustn't disappoint them,' he smirked.

Nick really had a knack for knowing what made people tick. This student was greedy as well as boastful. Also not too bright.

The boys played so badly, it was embarrassing. Chance was even more bumbling and pathetic than usual. Naturally, Loudmouth cleaned them out. But just as their victim got up from the table, Nick gave this hammy gasp of surprise.

'I quite forgot! I have my rent money hidden inside my shirt, for safekeeping. Would you do us the honour of playing again?' he pleaded.

I couldn't believe Loudmouth would fall for it. But like I said, he wasn't too bright. His eyes lit up with pure greed. 'Let's play for everything in our purses! And perhaps your luck will change?' he added, obviously thinking they were gluttons for punishment.

Their luck did change—dramatically. Nick and Chance revealed totally unsuspected gambling skills, and Loudmouth lost the lot, including the money he'd won from Nick and Chance.

Nick and his mates fled with their winnings, flushed with excitement.

'Smooth as cream,' Nick gloated. 'Here is your prize, Cat.'

Cat hastily stowed her share inside her bodice. Eek! I do hope she isn't turning into a gangster's moll, I thought anxiously.

Reuben sagged with relief. 'You were right, Mel. They pulled it off.'

'Looks like it,' I agreed.

Nick and Chance took Cat to the playhouse to celebrate.

We'd just joined this massive queue outside, when Nick frowned. 'I forgot my pomander,' he complained. 'I'm going to buy some oranges.' And he disappeared into the crowd.

Lola and Reuben exchanged baffled glances.

'Was that like, code?' said Lola.

I grinned. 'Haven't you noticed those fancy fashion items some people have hanging from their belts?'

'Those pepperpot thingies?' said Lola.

I nodded. 'Well, they're filled with incredibly strong perfume.'

(OK, so I might have read up on the Tudors a *teensy* bit. I mean, once you get into it, it's quite juicy!)

'OK,' Lola said cautiously. 'And Elizabethans do this because . . . ?'

'Because they have this theory that disease is caused by bad smells.'

Reuben pulled a face. 'And you can see why! Have you ever smelled so many unwashed humans in your life?'

Chance was wandering up and down the queue, chatting to various acquaintances. He had this incredible ability to get on with people from all walks of life. One minute he was talking about fetlocks to a groom, then minutes later I heard him swapping leather-making jargon with someone.

'Your boy's networking,' I giggled to Reuben.

'My boy's a total chameleon, more like,' he sighed.

When Chance rejoined her, Cat gave him one of her looks. 'You are the strangest boy,' she said. 'You write like an Oxford scholar, yet you never know where your next meal is coming from. Don't you ever want to follow a trade like a normal person?'

Chance looked appalled. 'Seven years working for the same master? The same work day after day, for no wages? Every day the same?' He shuddered. 'I'd rather you sent for the constables and had me thrown in Newgate jail.'

'But what will become of you?' Cat said in an anxious voice.

His eyes grew hazy with worry. 'I don't know. I wake at night in a sweat, wondering why I was—'

But he was interrupted by a blare of noise. An actor from the playhouse was blowing loud blasts on a trumpet—our signal to go in.

68

Nick caught up with his friends, tossing an orange to each of them as they filed in through the great carved doors. They rubbed the peel on the insides of their wrists, solemnly sniffing the perfume.

'Oh, *I* get it,' grinned Lola. 'Smart move.'

I'd only been to the theatre once before, on a school trip. It didn't leave much impression to be honest. I just remember miles of carpet and v. hard seats, which we had to sit on for like, hours.

Well, there was no carpet at the Lion. And the roof had a massive hole cut into it. You could actually see clouds floating overhead!

I'd assumed our kids' tickets would entitle them to seats, in this swanky grandstand affair at the side. But that cost an extra penny apparently (like, wow!). So we stood out in the open, with all the other hard-up folk. Groundlings, as you're meant to call them.

The posh patrons, lords and ladies and so on, had the spiffiest seats at the side of the stage. Actually, I think the groundlings enjoyed looking at them as much as the show.

At last several actors bounded on. The play had started.

To begin with, the audience didn't seem too fussed. They went on wandering about, chatting and cracking hazelnuts. But I was gripped. The play was nothing like my school experience. It was wild! Like circus and stand-up, pantomime and soap opera all jumbled together. Boys dressed as girls, actors nattering to the audience, and whenever things threatened to get heavy, the fool got everyone laughing again.

As it went on, the audience became totally involved, booing the villains, or screaming at the heroine to be careful. During a weepy bit near the end, a woman behind me was actually sobbing out loud.

'I always forget how much I love plays,' Cat whispered to Chance.

'I could have a job here, if I wanted,' he said at once.

'Here we go,' sighed Reuben.

Cat looked impressed. 'Really?'

'We could go backstage. I know some of the actors.'

'Oh, yes?' said Cat sharply. 'What name do *they* know you by?'

I couldn't help laughing. And then for some reason I glanced casually at the gorgeously dressed lords and ladies at the side of the stage, and my entire world went blurry.

There, sniffing his pomander and one hundred percent visible to the human race, was my number one cosmic enemy.

The last time I'd seen this particular PODS agent, he'd been wearing a T-shirt and jeans. But apart from his bleached hair, the figure up on the stage could have stepped out of an Elizabethan painting. And I know this sounds stupid, but I was hypnotised by his jewellery—huge knuckleduster rings with great winking stones. I couldn't take my eyes off them.

Omigosh! I'd better warn the others, I thought.

But suddenly this seemed like a really dangerous thing to do.

What if it isn't him? I panicked.

What if it's just some genuine Elizabethan aristocrat who only *looks* like him?

Check the eyes, Mel, I told myself. The agent had those scary dead eyes, remember?

So I had another frantic peek. And found myself looking at an empty seat.

I was totally confused. Had I just imagined the whole thing? Mr Allbright always said time-travel can play tricks with your mind.

The play finished in a storm of applause.

Nick gave a loud yawn. 'At last!' he said irritably. 'I thought it was going on for ever.'

He began to hurry his mates towards the exit. 'Come on! Those apprentices over there are spoiling for a fight and I don't want Cat mixed up in it.'

'I was going to take her backstage,' Chance protested.

But as usual Nick got his own way.

Outside, the weather was changing for the worse. Clouds were blowing up from the river, swallowing the last of the sunset, making it seem much later than it really was.

Looking back, I know I should have told the others what I'd seen. But I mean, an actual PODS up on the stage in full view, blatantly interacting with humans? How likely was that? And how come my mates didn't see him? It's not like I was the only angel in the area.

Much better keep quiet, Mel, I decided. If you make a big deal out of this, you'll only embarrass yourself.

Since we'd left the playhouse, Chance had been trudging along, smiling to himself. Suddenly he looked dismayed. 'We're almost at London Bridge!'

'Oh, so we are,' said Nick, as if he'd only just noticed.

'Why did we come this way?' said Chance. 'Cat said she had to go home.'

'Yes,' said Cat accusingly. 'What's your game, Nick Ducket?'

Nick touched one of her springy fuse-wire curls, and gave her his special smile. 'I just thought, that since Lady Fortune has been smiling on us . . .'

'No, no, NO,' said Cat. 'I said I'd

help you ONCE, Nick. I told you, my aunt is expecting me back.'

'Come, Cat,' Nick coaxed. 'You know you have a natural gift for deception, like all your—'

He broke off in surprise. A raggedy procession was heading our way. Men, women, apprentices and children, all pointing and laughing.

I heard the wavery tooting of a flute, a clunky little drum, explosive cracks like gunshots.

As they got closer, I saw that the musicians were just dirty little kids with scared expressions. Close behind was their dad, grinning all over his face and cracking a long whip. That's why I'd thought I heard gunshots. He wore a sleeveless leather jerkin, exposing his muscly arms and most of his hairy chest.

'Ooer, it's Mister Muscles the Lion Tamer!' I joked.

Lola muttered, 'That man's got more teeth than a shark!'

But Reuben didn't say a word. He'd gone totally white.

He'd seen the dancing bear.

CHAPTER SIX

I have never seen anything so sad as that bear trying to waltz. It was basically a bag of bones in a saggy fur coat, blind in one eye and covered with scars.

For some reason, it kept peering wistfully into faces in the crowd. It seemed to be looking for someone.

A shiver of wonder went through me. *Omigosh! It's looking for us!*

Unlike his bear, Mister Muscles was not a sensitive being, so it didn't occur to him there were angels in his vicinity. He had no idea why his beast was disobeying him, and he didn't care.

He cracked his whip violently, and the bear collapsed on to all fours. The crowd roared.

Chance had abruptly taken himself off down an alleyway. He seemed to be having a major argument with himself. For the first time since I'd known him, his thoughts jumped out at me.

I could seize his whip, break it into

pieces. But I'm not as strong as he is. I'll just make a fool of myself and the beast will be no better off.

Like some dazed sleepwalker, Reuben started walking towards the bear.

'Don't do anything!' I yelled. 'Don't do a *thing*!'

He did, though. Reuben did something I totally didn't expect.

He *spoke* to the bear in the most beautiful language I have ever heard. Actually, the soft mysterious sounds reminded me very slightly of that heavenly music, my cosmic lullaby.

When it heard these lullaby words, the bear grew very still. Very deliberately, it looked at Reuben with its one good eye, and Reuben looked back. And without worrying about its fleas, not to mention its smell (which was rank), Reuben put his arms around the bear. The bear looked totally blissful.

But Mister Muscles was desperate to get his show back on the road, so he started striking the bear with his whip again and again.

And to my horror, each time the whip cracked, Reuben groaned and doubled up. I couldn't understand what was happening. I mean, humans can't injure angels. Everyone knows that.

Lola was quicker on the uptake. She was already running towards him. 'The stupid boy's taking its pain, Mel!' she shrieked.

Five times the man struck at the bear, and each time Reuben almost fell. But on the sixth blow, someone caught the bear-keeper's arm in midair.

'I think it's had enough!' said a voice.

Everyone gasped, including me and Lola.

Nick calmly took the whip from Mister Muscles and my knees went to pure jelly with gratitude. Not only had he saved the bear, he'd saved my friend!

Nick might be a control freak, but he's a born leader, I thought admiringly. He can just walk into any situation and change it to suit himself.

I could actually feel the crowd switching loyalties. Beside Nick, Mister Muscles just looked like a cowardly bully. Suddenly nobody wanted anything to do with him. People began drifting away, muttering.

We rushed over to Reuben, but he insisted he was fine.

Nick smiled at Mister Muscles. 'It's almost nightfall. Rest and let the beast rest too. And feed your little cubs while you're about it. They look as if they need it.' He tossed some coins to Mister Muscles, who sullenly stowed them in his jerkin.

We watched the sad little circus trail down the alley to put up at The Fleece. Chance rejoined his mates, v. shame-faced.

Cat was glowing. 'Nick, you were wonderful. That poor bear!'

We thought he was wonderful too. This was the *real* Nick. The boy Lola had watched sleeping. The boy with beautiful dreams.

'You see, Lollie,' I whispered. 'It's working. He's improving already!'

Nick's eyes slid away from Cat's. 'We'd better walk you home,' he sighed. 'Unless you erm, changed your mind?' He gestured wistfully towards

78

the gaming house.

I don't believe you, Nick Ducket, I thought.

Cat gave him a mischievous smile. 'Oh well. Since I'm sure to get a beating, I may as well stay out and make a profit!'

She seemed genuinely cheerful, but I was confused. I just didn't get Nick. Moments ago, he'd done a genuinely good deed. But it was like he couldn't resist cashing in.

Lola's right, I thought miserably. He's always on the make.

Cat suddenly noticed Chance. 'Where have you been hiding?' she laughed. 'You should have seen Nick! He actually took that oaf's whip away!'

Chance forced a smile. 'I saw the whole thing. I wanted to stop him myself,' he added apologetically, 'but I—'

'But you were puking your guts up,' Nick grinned. 'We know.'

'Well, I'm fully recovered now and I'm VERY hungry!' Chance rubbed his belly, making fun of himself. 'Didn't I see a pieman somewhere?'

'Just around the corner,' said Cat promptly. 'Maybe he's still there.' She ran off, jingling coins.

The minute she'd disappeared, Chance said urgently, 'Nick, let's walk Cat home, then perhaps she won't get a beating. We've won enough for today.'

Nick's eyes grew cold. 'Enough for you, perhaps. I am a gentleman with a gentlemen's expenses.'

'Wouldn't your father help?' Chance asked tentatively. 'You're not the first person to get into debt.'

'How would you know?' Nick sneered. 'Without me, you'd probably be starving in the gutter. Yet when I ask for help, it's different.'

I couldn't believe he was being so horrible. I'd want to punch anyone who spoke to me like that. But Chance just stood there, taking it. 'Nick, you know I'd do anything,' he began.

And at that moment Lola said urgently, 'Mel! We've lost Reuben!'

*   *   *

We found our buddy in a squalid shelter in the tavern courtyard, giving the bear some angel TLC. He was singing under his breath as he tended its wounds. 'You're not alone,' he sang.

'You never told us you spoke bear,' Lola said softly.

'It's not exactly bear,' Reuben answered. 'It's this language angels invented at the dawn of creation, to communicate with animals.'

The bear gave Reuben a jealous nudge.

'He wants to come back with us,' he explained. 'I told him it's not his time.'

The bear hung its head as if it understood.

On top of everything else, this was too much for Lola. Tears spilled down her face.

'Don't cry, Lollie. It'll be all right,' I comforted her. Though I wasn't sure if I meant the bear, Nick's appallingly selfish behaviour, or the ultimate success of our cosmic fact-finding trip.

'But it looks so lonely,' she wept.

'His name is Sackerson,' Reuben

corrected her. 'And he's a very wise soul.'

By the time we'd dragged Reuben back to the gambling house, Cat had already lined up victim number two. She brought him over to the boys table, desperately trying to keep a straight face, but at the last minute someone barred their way.

'I'm Big Ned,' he slurred. 'And this game is mine.'

He sat down heavily, almost missing the chair. The boys grinned. A drunk was even better! And this one had obviously been drinking for hours. He kept dozing off and the boys had to wake him to take his turn. He still won, of course.

But just as Nick was psyching himself up for the final phase of their sting, Big Ned had an alarming personality change. His lids lost their drunken droop and this cold little gleam appeared in his eyes.

He picked up the cards, shuffling so fast, it sounded like pigeons taking off. And with a flick of his wrist, he sent all fifty-two cards streaming through the air in a perfect arc.

Cat's eyes went wide with alarm. 'Run!' she hissed.

Two burly men appeared, grinning like crocodiles.

'Bad luck, young tuns,' Ned said cheerfully. 'Tell you what, we'll play again. Maybe Lady Fortune will smile on you.'

Nick was grey with shock. 'We have no money!'

I recognised the 'Find The Lady' con-man among Ned's heavies. 'You haven't forgotten the rent money you put inside your shirt?' he said in his silky Irish voice. 'Aah, well. Rufus here will help you find it.'

'These have to be the resident crooks,' Lola whispered.

'Yeah and I don't think they appreciate amateurs on their turf,' I whispered back.

'We seen what you were up to this morning, young sirs,' said Ned in the same cheerful tone. 'Rufus wanted a little chat, didn't you, Rufus?'

Rufus glared, clenching his huge hands into fists.

Suddenly Ned grabbed Nick's doublet, jerking him to his feet. 'So now you're back, I think we'll have that private chat after all. Down by the river, where it's nice and quiet.'

The Fleece regulars seemed to know all about Ned's private chats. No-one even glanced up as the kids were bundled out into the yard.

It was pitch black, and the rain was hammering down again. All you could hear was rain and the river lapping invisibly nearby.

I was worried obviously, but not too worried. I was waiting for Nick to do his stuff, to turn the whole thing to his advantage, like he always did.

Only this time, he didn't.

It was like all his rich boy's confidence had suddenly deserted him. I've got this theory that he couldn't swim, because he started pleading with the men not to throw him in the river. He actually threw himself on his knees, whimpering like a little kid.

But the crooks calmly removed Nick's expensive shirt and doublet, saying he wouldn't need them where he was going.

Don't think we were hanging around like shiny Christmas decorations, while all this was going on. We were beaming vibes like crazy.

But absolutely nothing happened. Unless you count Rufus getting the torch to light finally. Now that they could see where they were going, the crooks began to hustle their captives across the courtyard towards the river.

They're going to die, I thought. Omigosh, they're really going to die!

And I completely freaked out.

'DO something, you idiot!' I screamed. 'You're going to drown!' And I actually whacked poor Chance between the shoulder blades.

WHOOSH! A jolt of angel electricity sizzled down my fingers.

Chance jumped as if he'd been zapped with a cattle prod.

Lola was horrified. 'Melanie! *Wake* them, we said, not shock the sassafras out of them!'

'I was upset,' I wailed.

'Shush,' hissed Reuben. 'Something's happening!'

It's hard to describe how Chance changed. It was something in his eyes. Suddenly, they looked like angel eyes. This was Chance, but not as we knew him. It was Chance minus his fog. And he was not about to let anyone die.

'Murder us if you must,' he said calmly. 'But spare my lady, for she is not of woman born.'

Big Ned stopped dead. 'What say you, boy?'

'Human attendants are easily replaced,' Chance explained. 'But if you harm my lady, her people may deal harshly with you.'

'Her people? You mean the Good Folk?' The Irishman almost whispered the words. He glared at Ned. 'You swore she was a blackamoor.'

Chance gave a chilling chuckle. 'Are you blind? Have you not seen her eyes? They are as green as willows in spring.'

The con-man thrust the torch towards Cat. What he saw made his hand shake. 'Elf fire!' he hissed.

There was a pricklingly tense silence while Cat tried to look cold and

86

heartless, like an elf king's daughter.

'See how she looks at you?' said Chance. 'Would a mortal look at her captors so brazenly? But we should not talk of such things in the dark, only . . .'

'Only what?' barked Big Ned, sounding panic-stricken.

'Only, if my lady should let down her hair, run for your lives.'

'What will happen?' whispered Rufus, completely under Chance's spell.

'Her father will appear in the guise of . . .' Chance let his voice tail off.

'Tell us, boy!' Ned pleaded. 'In what shape will he appear?'

Cat had figured out what Chance was up to by this time. She began to hum dreamily. And as she hummed, she slowly removed her cap, letting her fuse-wire curls fall dramatically around her shoulders.

Rufus's eyes bulged. *'She's calling him!'* he hissed.

But it was really Reuben who saved the day. Just as I twigged that Cat was humming Sackerson's waltz, our brilliant buddy called out in that skin-pricklingly lovely angel language.

Only it didn't sound like a lullaby this time. It sounded like a war-cry.

Sackerson's sleep was already disturbed by the tune which tortured his daylight hours. Reuben's summons did the rest. With a great roar, the bear rose up out of the darkness.

Dropping the torch, the crooks fled, howling with terror.

A micro-second later, the bear ran out of chain and sat down heavily, scratching its bottom.

Cat was delirious. 'Chance! It is you who have elfin blood, enchanting them with that wild tale!'

He hugged her. 'What about you? You remembered its tune!'

'It just floated into my head,' she said excitedly. 'That poor beast did the rest.'

Nick just stood watching, kind of flaring his nostrils and trying to look superior. Not easy to pull off, when you're shirtless and shivering in the rain.

Without a word, Chance whipped off his battered doublet and held it out to Nick.

Nick pulled a face. 'Ugh, it smells of sweat and onions.'

Cat totally exploded. 'How dare you be so high and mighty, Nick Ducket?' she yelled. 'If it wasn't for Chance, we might all have died!'

She was practically in tears.

'Well, I have learned my lesson,' she went on more quietly. 'And I pray you have learned yours. For I fear this reckless life will be the death of you.'

Nick studied his boots for a second. Then he gave her one of his winning smiles. Not his usual five-star variety, but a smile nonetheless.

'Everything you say is true,' he said, to my surprise. 'And I promise I will turn over a new leaf. I had been thinking of going up to Oxford, which would make my father very happy. And maybe one day I will write plays. Yes,' Nick said dreamily. 'I think I would enjoy that.'

Chance beamed. 'If I take that job at the playhouse, maybe I can act in them!'

But Nick didn't answer him and

there was an uneasy silence.

He's ashamed, I thought. If it wasn't for Chance, Nick would be floating in the river, and he knows it.

Chance was staring wistfully at his best mate, desperate to get things back on their old easy footing.

And all at once he started doing this silly walk, imitating the fool at the Lion. He did it brilliantly and it worked like a charm. In no time, Nick was roaring with laughter.

But I had to turn away. Ten minutes ago, Chance's eyes had blazed with cosmic intelligence. Now he was Nick's fool again. It was like watching Sackerson trying to waltz.

Still laughing, Nick draped his arms round his friends' shoulders. 'Let us swear to be friends for ever! For you are the most faithful friends anyone ever had.'

Cat laughed. 'We swear!'

Nick snatched up the torch and they walked off, with Chance capering beside them, shouting, 'We swear, we swear, oh great master!'

I started to follow them but Lola

said softly, 'It's over, Mel.'

I felt a funny ache in my chest. 'Are you sure?'

Nick's laughing voice floated back. 'What about this for a stage direction, Chance? "Exit: pursued by a bear"!'

And at that moment, as if someone had turned off a tap, the rain stopped and a big silvery moon came from behind the clouds. The scene had Happy Ending written all over it. Everyone was happy except me. But I totally didn't know why.

Reuben took my hand. 'Ready?'

I stiffened. I'd heard the tiniest movement in the dark. 'Did you hear that?'

'Rats,' shuddered Lola. 'Come on. Let's get back to civilization! 'Bye, Sackerson,' she called. 'We won't forget you.'

The bear closed his eyes as the beam of light came strobing down.

And with a whoosh of cosmic energy, we went zooming home.

CHAPTER SEVEN

On the way back, Reuben kept closing his eyes as if he felt dizzy. But when I asked if he was OK, he snapped, 'Why shouldn't I be?'

I know now that I should have checked it out, but I was preoccupied with worries of my own. I had a bad feeling we hadn't found Michael's glitch after all. And lurking beneath that worry was a worse fear. I was scared our humans might be in danger.

I tried telling Lola, but she didn't want to know.

'Could you drop it, Mel?' she pleaded. 'I want to get home, have a couple of hours' sleep, then grab my dancing shoes! Hey, I can't wait to go to that new place, The Babylon Café.'

When Lollie starts babbling, like a girl who's had too many mochaccinos, it's her way of saying, 'I'm freaking out inside, but I can't talk about it yet, OK?'

So it was a big relief when the door slid open and rays of lovely celestial light flooded in.

'I can't wait to tell Michael,' Lola bubbled.

Then her face crumpled. Our welcome party consisted of one person. Al, the maintenance guy.

'Mike's sorry, but something came up,' he mumbled shyly.

Lola stared around the deserted Arrivals area in bewilderment. 'But Michael *always* comes to meet us!'

I didn't feel too cheerful myself. I really look forward to that moment when I see Michael hurrying towards us, like he can't wait to hear every detail of our trip. Him *not* being there made everything feel unreal. As if part of me was still out there, adrift in time.

Al shrugged. 'Mike was archangel on call, so what can you do?' He gave a bashful glance in my direction. 'You'll never guess where he's gone.' (Al and I have this little running joke.)

'Don't tell me,' I sighed. 'He had to bale out my century again.'

Al faked amazement. 'Incredible!

93

How'd you know?'

I grinned. 'A wild hunch!'

'Is it me, or was Al acting strange just now?' Reuben asked in his new tired voice, as we headed home in the limo.

Lola gave him her party-girl smile. 'It's you, Sweetpea. He was trying to make up for Michael not being there, that's all.'

I didn't have the energy to talk, so I just gazed out of the limo, watching familiar landmarks flow past.

Suddenly Reuben tapped on the glass between us and the driver.

'Can you drop me off at the dojo?'

Lola looked astonished. 'Are you sure? You look like you need some rest.'

'Pure angels don't need to rest,' he said huffily. 'A complete work-out, that's all I need.'

I didn't think Reuben looked up to a martial arts work-out either. But you can't tell boys anything, so we promised to meet him at Guru next morning. Guru is our favourite hang-out and serves the best breakfasts in

94

the universe.

'My treat,' I reminded him. 'I've got ID now, remember.'

On the way back to our dorm, I caught sight of myself in the driver's mirror and hastily fluffed out my hair. Then I began to brush down my jacket. You are *such* a muck-magnet, Mel, I scolded myself. Where *did* all these hairs come from?

I examined one closely and felt a pang. A few of Sackerson's bear hairs had hitched a ride back to Heaven. And I had that weird floaty feeling again, as if I'd left an important part of me behind.

Several hours later I still couldn't sleep. Without knowing how I got there, I found myself over by the window, gazing out over the twinkling lights of the city.

Heavenly architects are something else. Even super-modern buildings are awesome here—glittering hi-tech domes and soaring skyscrapers.

'Aren't you thrilled to be back in this beautiful city, Mel?' I said aloud. 'You can go back to doing all that fun stuff with your mates.'

But I couldn't seem to remember what that stuff was. I could only think of all those long nights down at Angel Watch. Which set me off thinking about my mum and my little sister, Jade. If only I could let them know how much I loved them . . .

Then it hit me. 'Oh, you little devil!' I scolded myself. *'That's* why you took all those night shifts! You were hoping the Beeby family would flash up on your screen one night!'

Under normal conditions, I'd have been shocked at myself. But part of me was floating in time, and all of me was exhausted, and absolutely nothing felt real.

Go to bed, Mel, I told myself. In the morning things will look better.

And I lay down on my economy-sized bed, and killed the lights.

*   *   *

You couldn't call it a dream exactly. It was more like a movie trailer. Three Elizabethan teenagers running through

96

the rain, laughing and joking. There were gold sparkles dancing in the air, all mixed up with the rain and the night, and I heard myself saying, 'Aren't fifty-fifty set-ups the dangerous kind?'

Then the trailer cut out and a new one started, almost identical to the first. Only for some reason there weren't so many sparkles, and the streets were darker and way more menacing.

I don't know how many times I had to watch that scene. Each time it got darker and more nightmarish. Even the rain was scary, thundering down overflows, flooding into rain barrels and puddles, crashing and slooshing. And suddenly I couldn't stand it. I sat up gasping for breath, my heart pounding.

I realised someone was tapping on my door. 'It's me, Reuben.'

I got up and let him in.

He was still in his baggy martial-arts gear and worryingly pale around the edges.

'Sorry, I know it's late.' Reuben half-fell into my armchair, then winced and prised a leather boot out from under his behind.

'I hate to say this,' he said, 'but I've got the feeling we lost the plot back there.'

'Me too.' I told him all about my horror-movie trailer.

Reuben closed his eyes. 'This isn't good,' he said. 'We must have tipped the cosmic balance the wrong way.'

I was horrified. 'But how? I mean—'

Lola stumped in, with a flamingo-pink robe thrown over her PJs, her curls sticking up like radio antennae. 'Could you keep it down?' she grumbled.

'Are we bothering you?' I said apologetically.

'Yeah, with your stupid negative thoughts.' Lola dumped herself down on my rug. 'Plus I was already being bothered by my stupid negative thoughts,' she admitted grumpily.

Reuben reached over and ruffled her hair. 'Let's hear them. The stupid negative thoughts of Lola Sanchez.'

Lola began ticking them off on her

fingers. 'One, Michael wasn't there to meet us. He's *always* there. Two, Al was tying himself in knots, using every word in his vocabulary, except "You blew it, kids". Three, I ran into Amber in the hall and she totally didn't know what to do with herself when she saw me.'

'Four,' Reuben interrupted. 'It was just the same at the dojo. I started to feel like I didn't even exist.'

'FIVE,' Lola said loudly, 'I feel as if we've just made a big mistake. I can feel it, in here.' She thumped her chest.

I was horrified. 'You honestly think Michael is giving us the cold shoulder because we screwed up our mission? He'd never do that.'

'It's not like they're punishing us,' said Reuben. 'More giving us the space to figure things out for ourselves.'

'Oh,' I said.

But none of us had the slightest idea what we'd done wrong.

'Oh, well. We can't do anything until Michael gets back,' Lola sighed. 'We should get some sleep.'

'I'm staying up, thanks,' I shuddered. 'I'm not risking that horror movie again.'

And then, with a feeling like going down too fast in a lift, I had a chilling thought.

What if our depressing homecoming had something to do with my weird hallucination at the playhouse?

What if my imaginary PODS agent was real?

I was flooded with panic. Omigosh, Mel, I think you just screwed up BIG time.

I've got to tell them, I thought. I've got to tell them now!

But I couldn't make my voice work properly. 'Lollie,' I croaked. 'Remember our first field-trip when I rescued the little kid in the air raid?'

'Do I! Reubs, you should have heard her yell at Orlando! She—'

I was desperately talking over her. 'Remember that PODS guy?'

'Your gorgeous bad boy look-alike? What about him?'

I described how I'd seen him at the playhouse, passing himself off as human.

Lola almost went into orbit. 'You're kidding! You saw him *again*?'

I buried my face in my hands. 'I wasn't sure if I was imagining it. I am so STUPID.'

Reuben's eyes had closed again. 'Don't beat yourself up, Mel,' he said in a tired voice.

'Why does it have to be me? Why didn't you guys see him?'

'Maybe it's you he's after, babe,' Lola explained.

I felt myself turn cold. 'Why? What have I done to him?'

'Who knows how their minds work,' Reuben said, without opening his eyes.

But while Reuben was talking, I was mentally replaying those vital last seconds on Earth. The stealthy sounds in the darkness—that was the PODS too. He'd love to think of me remembering it when it was too late.

Then I thought, but maybe it's *not* too late.

And a weird thing happened. All my fear and self-pity fell away. As if I was looking down from some high mountain peak somewhere, and seeing everything with total clarity.

It's not that I stopped being scared. More that I saw our situation incredibly calmly. As if I'd thrown a dice, and was about to make my next move in some vast cosmic game, a game I totally didn't understand.

'We shouldn't have left those kids,' I told the others. 'Come on. We're going back.'

* * *

Al is a highly-trained professional, so if he was surprised when three trainee angels showed up in the middle of the night, demanding to be returned to Tudor times, he didn't let it show.

Actually, I got the feeling he was incredibly relieved. Not only that, but he had a portal all ready to go. He ran the usual checks, then I noticed him shuffling his shoes a bit.

'Look, I don't know how much Michael told you, but the fact is, we have a situation. Which means I can't beam you back through the exact same time-window. I got to send you through the nearest *available* window, OK?'

'Sounds mysterious,' said Lola.

Al lowered his voice. 'Like I say, we got a situation. Didn't you ever wonder why the Agency sent you in the first place?'

'Well, actually—' I began.

'The fact is, Michael didn't want to do it,' he said earnestly. 'But it was send you or no-one, know what I'm saying? The only reason you guys were able to slip through was because of some cosmic loop-hole they somehow overlooked.'

Reuben looked bewildered. 'The Agency overlooked something?'

'He means the Opposition, Sweetpea.'

Al looked queasy. 'I don't discuss those people. Some words leave a bad taste, if you get my meaning?'

He doled out our angel tags. We put them on, slightly stunned.

'Hey, did I mention you got to swap humans?' he called as we climbed into the portal. 'Sorry for any inconvenience, but it's Agency policy.'

And the last thing I saw through the

portal door was Al shyly giving us the thumbs-up, like he was saying, 'Better luck this time.'

CHAPTER EIGHT

We found ourselves in a crowd of happy, laughing Elizabethans. The soft chords of a lute drifted through the air. Everyone was carrying armfuls of white blossom. And from behind the houses and spires of London came the misty sound of a cuckoo.

Lola's face was a picture. 'Did we just land in the middle of a wedding?'

'I think it's some kind of May Day celebration,' I said.

Her eyes brightened. 'Like a fiesta?'

Reuben was enchanted. 'Do they do this in your century, Mel?'

'Erm, not where I come from,' I grinned.

And to prove this wasn't a total Disney experience, a woman opened a window and emptied a chamber pot into the street.

Our watches flashed and we made minor adjustments.

'Hey, they didn't split us up,' pointed out Reuben. 'That means our humans are in this crowd somewhere. I wonder who's got who this time?'

Lola's watch and mine both beeped. Seconds later, two familiar figures wandered past, holding hands.

And Lola went, 'I don't *believe* it!'

I didn't believe it either. Was this honestly the first time-slot the Agency could manage? This Cat was two years older at least, and stunningly pretty, with her curls falling loose and a crown of blossoms in her hair. And Chance looked better in every way—happier, healthier, and just generally more *there*, somehow. The zing in my chest told me that he was my responsibility this time.

I won't deny that it was deeply disturbing missing out on such a major chunk of their lives. Time-travel is weird like that. But I was so happy to see them safe after my scary premonitions, that I could have kissed them. 'Don't they look great?' I burbled. 'And they're actually an item! How about that!'

We soon found out that Cat and Chance were on their way to meet

Nick. This was more of a coincidence than it sounds. It seemed he'd been out of touch for months.

'He's longing to see you,' Chance was saying. 'He said he'd called into the Feathers several times but you're never there.'

'With his fine new friend. I know, Nettie told me.' Cat sounded wary.

'Nick is extremely fine himself, these days,' he admitted. 'I hardly recognised him when he came backstage. But he's exactly the same. A new sweetheart for every day of the week.'

'What did you talk about?' she said curiously.

'Oh, he had erm, a business proposition.' Chance sounded just a little too careless.

But Cat was blushing furiously. 'Did you tell Nick—you know?'

He beamed at her. 'He was happy for us. He said it was a pity the cause of true love did not always run so smooth.'

She frowned. 'That's a very strange thing to say.'

'You're so suspicious, Catherine

Darcy! Nick says you always think the worst of him. Let me go on with my tale. It's very tragic. Nick found one of the queen's ladies weeping in the garden. A beautiful lady apparently. Eventually Nick persuaded her to tell him her troubles.'

'I can imagine,' Cat said darkly.

'The lady made Nick swear to tell no-one—'

'Oh, no-one except you and me and Nettie and the town crier!'

Cat saw Chance's face. 'Sorry,' she said humbly. 'Tell your story.'

'It seems she is in love with a Spaniard, a very handsome one. But because of the climate at court, they cannot be seen speaking together.'

Cat's eyes widened. 'How sad! And how *silly*!'

'Isn't it?' said Chance eagerly. 'But Nick has thought of a plan to help her. Not only that, he says it's an opportunity for me to earn a great deal of money. There's no risk. He says I'd just be the go-between.'

Cat flung up her hands. 'And you *believed* him?'

We had reached a green space between the houses, where a maypole was decorated with spring flowers and coloured ribbons. Some young people were doing a skippy-type country dance to the sound of flutes and fiddles.

'It's true!' I heard Chance say. 'I'd be playing Cupid and making money at the same time. Money for us, Cat,' he coaxed. 'So we can be married!'

'People got married really young in these days,' I explained to Lola, who was looking v. shocked. 'Weird I know,' I added. 'I mean she's just a teenager, right? Why limit yourself?'

'You haven't seen Nick for months,' Cat was saying earnestly. 'Now suddenly he wants to help you. How do you know there's no risk? How do you know he doesn't wish you harm?'

Chance laughed. 'Because he's my friend.'

Cat opened her mouth, 'But—'

'No buts, Catherine Darcy,' he said firmly. 'It's May day, the sun is shining and I intend to dance with the most beautiful girl in London.'

And he swept her off to join the

dancers.

Lola shrugged. 'We must have been suffering from time-travel fatigue or something. They seem fine to me.'

'I'm not sure about this scheme of Nick's,' said Reuben doubtfully. 'Wasn't he going to university? I think he's my human this time, so—'

'Oh, who cares?' said Lola. 'He's doing well for himself. Now he's trying to help an old friend.'

'Yeah, but—'

'No buts!' she teased him. 'It's May day, the sun is shining and I intend to dance with the most beautiful Sweetpea in London!' And she danced away with him, giggling.

I watched the dancers dreamily, noticing that each time Cat and Chance met and linked arms, they smiled into each other's eyes, before whirling away in opposite directions. It kind of reminded me of how I feel with Orlando sometimes.

I came out of my thoughts with a jolt. Someone was standing beside me, a good-looking young man with a rose in his cap. Though I'd have probably recognised Nick without the rose, from his faintly superior smile.

He'd become incredibly stylish since the last time I'd seen him— slashed sleeves, gorgeous shoes. I was convinced the gold pomander hanging from his belt was studded with actual jewels.

Lola's right, I thought. All those dreams and dire premonitions, they were purely in my head!

There was a burst of clapping as Cat and Chance swung each other energetically between two rows of their fellow dancers.

I was watching Nick eagerly, waiting for him to recognise his old friends, so I saw the exact moment when his face changed.

And his eyes went totally cold.

Then he stepped forward, laughing, as they went hurtling past. And it was like nothing had ever happened.

But I knew it had. Nick might look the same, but I'd glimpsed a chilling stranger underneath. And I knew the danger in my dreams was real.

Reuben ran up, followed by Lola.

111

'According to my watch, Nick's around here somewhere,' he said breathlessly.

'Yeah,' I said. 'He is.'

Lola caught sight of him. 'Woo!' she said. 'He is doing well!'

It struck me that Reuben was looking feverish. His eyes were too bright and his face was much too pale.

'Are you sure you're OK?'

'Let's make a deal,' he said irritably. 'When I'm not, you'll be the first person I tell.'

Nick, Cat and Chance went off to a nearby tavern, with us following behind as close as shadows. They sat outside in the sunshine and Nick ordered ale and some kind of game pie.

'Now we can catch up on each other's news,' he beamed. But before Cat and Chance could even open their mouths, Nick launched into this juicy scandal involving all these major court celebrities.

'And you must come and visit me in my new rooms,' he said. 'They are really very fine. As different to my old place as night from day.'

'I liked your old place,' Cat said

quietly.

How's he *paying* for this? I thought. His family isn't *that* rich.

I didn't get the impression Nick actually worked for his living. Not in those sleeves.

I think Nick noticed that Cat wasn't as impressed as he'd hoped, because he suddenly said, 'And how is life treating my lovely Catherine?'

'Very well,' she said promptly and she totally couldn't prevent herself smiling at Chance. 'But I don't know any lords and ladies, so I have no interesting news to tell.'

Then her face lit up. 'Oh, but I've heard my father will soon be home from sea! I wonder if he'll recognise me,' she added anxiously. 'He's been away so long.'

'And you, Chance?' said Nick. 'How are you liking the theatrical life?'

'Very much,' said Chance eagerly. 'I never know what I'll be doing from one day to the next. One moment I'm helping actors learn their lines, the next taking care of the properties.'

'What are properties, exactly?' said

113

Nick in a bored tone.

'Almost anything! For instance, if the heroine dies tragically of snake bite, I must make sure the snake is to hand!'

'Oh,' said Nick. 'A real dogsbody.'

Cat looked annoyed. 'He will be an actor one day. Only last month, he took the part of the fool, when Will Kemp had the fever.'

Nick pulled a face. 'He'd had plenty of practice, I'll be bound.'

The entire angel contingent was squirming. It was like everything Nick said was designed to make Chance look like a total loser, compared to him.

'Chance, I must introduce you to this new friend of mine,' he said loftily. 'He could get you work as an actor tomorrow if I asked him. You don't need to do all this ridiculous fetching and carrying.'

Chance suddenly spotted a young actor from the playhouse. 'I've just got to ask Kit something,' he mumbled. I got the feeling Kit owed him money.

Cat looked distinctly dismayed at the idea of being alone with Nick. I think she knew he'd try to chat her up.

Didn't take him long either.

'Ah, Cat,' he sighed, giving her that special smile of his. 'When I think how you cared for me once.'

'Yes, I did, when I was a little girl,' Cat said pointedly. 'But I am grown up now, so I prefer a man who is not afraid of his own heart.'

Nick looked scornful. 'They say that love is blind. But how you can prefer this nobody—'

'Chance is not nobody!' she blazed.

'He doesn't even know his own name!' Nick sneered. 'What do you call someone who has neither wealth, power or influence?'

'I'm talking about hearts, Nick! And his heart is like a twin to mine.'

'Ah, I see! You are twin souls!' His voice was mocking.

'Yes. We are!'

She calmly held Nick's gaze, letting him know that his attempt to put Chance down had basically boomeranged.

He quickly pulled himself together. 'Then you must marry,' he said in his lordly way. 'Luckily I've put an excellent financial opportunity Chance's way.'

'I heard.' And suddenly Cat leaned over and put her lips really close to Nick's ear. 'Don't hurt him, Nick Ducket,' she said softly. 'Don't you dare.'

Chance reappeared, looking dejected. The actor had obviously fobbed him off.

Nick pushed back his chair. 'Come to my rooms tonight, Chance, and we'll talk business. Sorry to rush off. I've arranged to meet someone.'

Reuben got ready to leave too. For some reason this made me deeply uneasy.

'Maybe you should stay with us,' I said. 'I'm not sure you—'

'Melanie!' he warned. 'Nick's my human now. Agency policy, remember? I have to go.'

'He's right,' said Lola. 'He has to.' But she didn't look happy about it either.

I watched them walk away across the green. I thought Reuben looked terrifyingly fragile.

Cat and Chance were leaving as well. Cat's aunt needed her to help in the tavern.

I noticed that Lola seemed unusually depressed. 'I've really gone off Nick,' she blurted suddenly.

'Don't feel bad about it,' I told her. 'People change.'

'But you were right, Mel. He's not the glitch. Or if he is, he's only a little *part* of it. I'm so confused.'

I slipped my arm through hers. 'We're confused now,' I said. 'But when we see the light, we'll go, "Wow! Was that ALL?'

She giggled. 'You're such an idiot.'

We'd almost reached the Feathers when Cat said, 'Chance, I do wish you'd turn Nick's offer down. I don't trust him.'

Chance looked shocked. 'You're wrong. When I had nothing, Nick saved my life. He's a wonderful friend.'

'So he keeps telling you.' Cat's voice was pure acid. She took a breath. 'Nick did say one true thing. He says you don't know your name.'

For the first time since our return, I

saw Chance's eyes grow foggy with hurt. 'He's wrong,' he said.

'But your name's not Chance?' she said softly.

He didn't answer. She put her arms around him. 'Are you ever going to tell me?'

I was quite interested to know this myself, so I deliberately tried to pick up on Chance's thought vibes. But they were totally confused. Even with my angel senses, I couldn't figure out what was going on. I could just see this agonizing struggle going on inside him.

'I promise,' he said carefully, 'that if I tell my name to anyone, it will be to you.'

She laughed. 'You'll have to tell me when we get married!'

As we reached the Feathers, a grubby white labrador bounded out.

'Promise me one thing?' Cat pleaded, as she tried to stop the dog licking her face. 'Be careful of Nick's new friend.'

'That's very dramatic,' he teased her. 'Why do you say that?'

'I told you, he came to the tavern

with Nick. Nettie said Snowball took one look and went streaking out of the house, with his tail between his legs. She says he's the devil in disguise.'

Chance laughed. 'Nettie thinks all men are devils in disguise!'

Like a song from a distant car radio, Reuben's tune floated into my head. *'You're not alone, you're not alone . . .'*

With a prickle of fear, I saw Lola mouthing the same words.

I grabbed my angel tags. They were burning hot as the Angel Link kicked in.

'Reuben, are you OK?'

His voice was hardly audible. 'Mel, we got it wrong.'

'What? What are you saying?'

'A trap . . . a cosmic trap!'

'You're not making sense, Sweetpea,' said Lola urgently. 'Someone trapped you?'

There was a long terrible pause.

'Not me,' he got out. 'Chance . . . for Chance.'

'Reuben,' I pleaded. 'Are you hurt?'

But I could just hear the words 'been so stupid' and 'fight'.

'Omigosh!' I said. 'He's really hurt, Lollie! That means . . .'

'Reuben, try to hold on,' Lola told him. 'We're coming to get you.'

'. . . careful,' Reuben gasped. 'Edward . . .'

'Who the heck's Edward?' said Lola.

There was another long rasping pause.

'. . . Nick's friend. He's with the PODS.'

CHAPTER NINE

We found Reuben slumped in Nick's rooms. He tried to raise his head, but he was too weak. 'Sorry,' he muttered. 'Such a wuss.'

'You're going to be OK, Sweetpea,' Lola told him. 'We'll get you home.' But I heard her voice wobble.

Reuben's visible injuries were truly terrible, but the worst PODS damage is always deep down. It was like he'd been totally drained of all his beautiful angelic energy, like he was hardly Reuben any more.

It seemed as if we stayed like that for an eternity—Lola cradling Reuben's head in her lap, me softly stroking his hand. Then a white light strobed down and two heavenly paramedics appeared.

'Len, it's just a bunch of kids!' one exclaimed. 'How'd they get here?'

His mate immediately bent over Reuben. What he saw really shocked him. 'What on earth did they attack him with?' he muttered.

And suddenly I remembered those jewelled knuckledusters. The way I couldn't take my eyes off them.

I swallowed. 'There was only one agent. And I think it was his rings.'

The paramedic was mystified. 'This happened on a *research* trip?'

'Had to be,' his mate muttered back. 'No other cosmic personnel are allowed in.'

'So who attacked the kid?'

'Beats me. Let's just get them back home. Come on, girls.'

They were all ready to beam us all up. Lola and I exchanged panic-stricken looks.

'Thanks but we're staying.' I tried to sound crisp and professional.

'We can't allow that, miss. This is officially an angel no-go area.'

'Check it out with the Agency if you want,' said Lola fiercely. 'All I know is Michael gave us a job to do. Take care of our friend, OK?'

*   *   *

It felt incredibly lonely after they'd gone, and we both had a bit of a cry.

I was trying desperately to understand what was happening. Nothing seemed to make sense.

'Lollie,' I said tearfully. 'Have you ever heard of an angel-free zone?'

She shook her head. 'It's not just our lot that can't come in. All cosmic personnel, he said.'

'So how come that PODS guy is here?'

'Good question,' she sighed.

'So are we violating some cosmic treaty, just by being here?'

'I don't think so, Boo. Remember how Michael kept insisting it wasn't a mission? Officially we're kids on an educational trip. That way we don't pose a threat to the big guys.'

'Why didn't Michael explain?'

She frowned. 'I don't know. But he never does anything without a reason. You know that.'

'I know it in Heaven,' I admitted. 'Down here, you start to wonder.'

Lola gave me a searching look. 'Think you'll be OK by yourself? We really should check on Cat and Chance.'

The prospect of Lola going anywhere without me filled me with terror. I grabbed her hand. 'Lollie, can we actually do this?'

She pulled her hand away and jammed her thumbs in her belt loops. 'We're the cosmic musketeers,' she said fiercely. 'We don't give in and we don't give up. Got it?'

I swallowed hard. 'Got it.'

Lola touched her angel tags. 'Later.' And she vanished.

I was just about to beam myself to Chance when I heard someone cautiously lift the latch.

I practically went into orbit. *He's back! The PODS came back!*

Chance peered around the door. 'Nick? Oh, nobody here.'

I clutched my pounding heart. 'That's right, nobody here,' I said frantically. 'So let's get out of here while we still can.'

But Chance just ambled about, admiring Nick's pad. After he'd had a good nose round, he poured himself some ale, hacked a crust off a loaf he'd found under a cloth, then sat riffling through Nick's books, calmly chomping away.

'For Pete's sake!' I wailed.

But you can only panic for so long. An hour or so later, Chance was still riffling and I was nodding off.

Then for the second time I heard the metallic clunk of the latch. I totally broke out into goosebumps. And Nick walked in with his new best friend.

I could feel the PODS agent deliberately not looking at me.

'Ah, Chance, made yourself comfortable, I see!' said Nick in a forced tone. 'I don't think you've met my friend, Edward Brice.'

Chance jumped up, scattering crumbs, and went to shake hands.

Brice gave a frosty nod. 'It's a pleasure to make your acquaintance, sir. I'll make myself scarce,' he murmured to Nick. 'You two have business to discuss.'

I had to hand it to him. Brice had really done his homework. His speech, his Elizabethan manners, were perfect.

The bleached hair, however, was pure twenty-first century. That's because he'd borrowed it from my old school crush, along with his gorgeous face and the bad-boy walk.

He waited until Nick was explaining Chance's go-between duties to him, then he strolled over. 'Hi, Mel. How's it going?' he said softly.

Sometimes there's so much you want to say, it all gets jammed up inside, and absolutely nothing comes out.

Then I caught sight of those manicured fingers with their glittering rings, and what came out was pure rage.

'I'm so relieved you didn't damage your jewellery,' I said icily.

Brice laughed. His eyes were totally dead, just like I'd remembered. 'Admit it, Mel, you're out of your depth.'

'So are you going to bash me too?' I said. 'Or do you have some quaint PODS code about not hitting girls?'

'Oh, I've got other plans for you, Mel. Long-term plans.' Brice stretched himself out on a wooden settle. 'These are great times, aren't they?' he sighed.

'I am in my element!'

Fortunately I didn't have to lose any brain cells guessing what this element was, because he couldn't wait to tell me.

'Chaos!' he explained gleefully. 'You really should hang out at court some time, Mel. All those shadowy stone corridors! All those convenient tapestries for traitors to eavesdrop behind! It's a plotters' paradise—I love it!'

I remembered how Lola thought we'd beamed down in the middle of a wedding because everyone was so happy.

'You just see ugly things,' I said. 'You make me sick.'

'I see what's real, sweetheart. Oh, did you know Golden Boy over there sold Chance's soul to pay his debts? Of course, Nick doesn't know that's what I'm after.'

Listening to Brice has this numbing effect. After a while you want to give up, the way people fall asleep in the snow.

'You know what's tragic?' he said.

127

'Chance can't believe Nick would hurt him. That's his fatal flaw.' He shook with laughter.

On the other side of the room, Chance and Nick were coming to the end of their talk.

'Funny,' Brice mused. 'Chance would be dead if it wasn't for you. And by the time this is over, he'll wish he was.'

'Why are you doing this?' I said angrily. 'If he's such a nobody, why go to all this trouble to destroy him?'

His eyes glittered. 'Sweetheart, you'll never know!'

And his laughter followed us out into the night. I knew I should be thankful I was still in one piece. Brice could have finished me, if he'd wanted to. He appeared to be saving that treat for later. As if Chance and I were his sad little pawns, so he could do what he liked with us.

Yikes! I suddenly realised that I hadn't been listening to Nick and Chance 'discussing business'! I'd been too busy listening to that toe rag, Brice. What was going to happen now? A fine guardian angel you're turning out to be, Mel Beeby, I thought glumly.

I followed Chance down dark smelly side streets, until we reached the river. He was off on some evil little mission for Nick, I realised with a lurch.

'The palace, Greenwich,' he muttered to a passing ferryman, who took him on board.

The palace! This was getting fishier by the minute!

It was pitch black out on the river, except for little glints and flashes where the ripples caught the moonlight, and the orangey flicker of the boatman's torch.

Sometimes a ferryboat slid past like a ghost. Most carried only one passenger, shadowy shapes in cloaks. I found myself shivering, and wondered if these were the evil conspirators Brice was talking about.

When we reached the other side, Chance gave the ferryman some coins. 'Wait for me, and you'll have the rest when I return,' he promised.

As soon as we left the river, he went zooming off into the undergrowth, making his way through the trees until we came out in some kind of park. Finally, we arrived at the rear of a huge building, which I assumed was the royal palace. Like everything else, it was in total darkness.

Chance tapped softly at a side-door. It opened slightly and he handed a crackly roll of parchment to whoever was on the other side. I saw a green silk-gloved hand give him another in exchange.

The instant the door closed, Chance went racing back through the park. His thoughts jumped out at me. *So much money for so little work! I'll just take this to Don Rodriguez and I'll get my first payment!*

As we sped back across the Thames in the dark, I could feel Chance smiling beside me. It made me want to cry.

'Wake up!' I whispered. 'I don't know why Brice has it in for you, but you've got to be ready for him, Chance. You've got to fight back.'

*   *   *

The next few days were the most stressful of my angel career.

Chance was leading a double life, and unfortunately I had to lead it with him. Lola and I mostly had to catch up via Angel Link.

'So when am I going to see you?' she said in despair one afternoon, her voice bouncing back at me like a bad mobile connection.

'I wish I knew.'

I was talking from the playhouse. Two actors in holey tights were leaping on and off boxes, practising sword fighting skills.

'I'm not saying Chance has like, criminal tendencies,' Lola was saying. 'But I do think he gets a buzz out of this cloak-and-dagger stuff.'

I felt despairing. 'Lollie, I don't think I'm the right person to help him. Maybe we should swap.'

Lola's voice crackled over the Link. 'You're doing fine. Oops, gotta go!' And she'd gone.

'I am SO not doing fine, Lollie,' I whispered miserably.

The trap was closing in. I knew it.

131

I sensed it as Chance went snaking between the trees in the dark. I knew it from the way I leapt out of my skin at the slightest twig crack. Details jumped out at me, like clues in a thriller. I didn't know what they meant, but I passed them on to Chance just the same.

'Don't you think it's suspicious, how they always wear the same gloves?' I told Chance one night. 'It might be just the one glove, actually. You only see one hand after all. Don Rodriguez's is wine-coloured. Though you'd think a Spanish nobleman could afford nicer leather. Hers is icky green silk. In my century we associate that colour with poison, hint hint.'

The brainwashing was Lola's idea. 'It's the dripping tap technique,' she explained during one of our chats. 'Repeat the same thing over and over and it's got to get through eventually.'

So I badgered Chance non-stop. 'How come such a noble lady only owns one pair of gloves? Come on, Cupid, how likely is that? She's probably just a maid. I bet Nick and

Brice are paying her to pose as a lady in waiting. If you ask me, this lovesick lady thing is pure fiction.'

By this time, we were at the house with the grand gates where Don Rodriguez lived.

'Chance, would you please stop being Robin Hood for one minute and check out the gloves!' I pestered. 'Because if the Don is wearing wine-coloured leather tonight, I think you should open that letter and see what's inside. Wake up and open your eyes, Chance. Open your eyes!'

I can't say for sure that Lola's technique worked. I can only tell you what happened.

At first it was business as usual. Chance went through a little side-gate, and tapped at a leaded window. I hated that window. It always stuck. And tonight it seemed to grate open with an especially edgy sound. As usual, a leather-gloved hand appeared.

And suddenly Chance's expression changed. He looked, *really* looked at the glove, as if he was seeing it in huge cinematic close-up.

Then he and Don Rodriguez exchanged crackly letters in the usual way, and Chance set off through the dark. I heard him muttering. 'Those gloves. Always the same colour and the leather is such poor quality . . .'

'Oh, *finally*!' I said.

But once again Chance was arguing with himself. 'I ferry their letters from one side of the river to the other, and I have no idea what is in them. But Nick would never betray me. Would he?'

A solitary linkman passed by. London streets were dangerous after dark, so people hired linkmen, big tough blokes with lamps, to make sure they got home safely. Chance called out, 'May I borrow your lamp?' followed by the usual chink of coins. 'Could you hold it up?' he asked. 'I have to read this important letter.'

The linkman grinned. 'A love letter, no doubt.'

Chance broke the seal on the parchment and scanned the letter frantically. 'It can't be true,' he whispered.

The linkman looked sympathetic.

'Given you the cold shoulder, has she? Oh, steady now, young sir, steady, lean on me!'

But I'd snooped over Chance's shoulder. And I knew the message in this letter was far deadlier than some teenage brush-off.

*　　　*　　　*

When Chance and I finally reached the Feathers, it was almost dawn. He stood throwing stones up at Cat's window for ages, but I think she must have been in a really deep sleep. In the end I called Lola up on the Link and told her to wake Cat up. Finally Cat appeared at the door, dazed and blinking in her nightshift, a stump of candle flickering in her hand.

'They have betrayed me!' Chance gasped. 'This letter says I am involved in a Spanish plot to kill the queen!'

Lola peeped out from behind Cat. 'Mel, what's going on?'

'The dripping tap,' I said feebly. 'I think it worked.' Lola threw her arms around me and we gave each other a big hug.

A burly, weatherbeaten man joined us in the doorway.

His beard had sprouted a few more grey hairs since I last saw him. Otherwise Cat's dad looked exactly the same, even down to the pearl earring.

He gave Chance a shrewd and very thorough looking-over.

'Catherine,' he said. 'This boy needs a shot of rum.'

* * *

I don't condone piracy obviously, but there are definite advantages to having a pirate in the family. Assuming they're on your side, that is. Once Cat's dad had heard Chance's story, he was totally on his side. Plus he came up with some v. colourful suggestions for getting Nick back, mostly involving gizzards and slitting of various kinds.

In a funny way, I think it helped Chance come to terms with what had just happened. It showed him that even though his best friend had betrayed him, there were people who really cared about him.

And though his eyes were still shocked, they weren't vague or foggy. Actually, I got the definite sense that old foggy Chance had gone for good.

And all at once he said in a totally steady voice, 'Cat, could you fetch me some paper and ink? I'm going to write a letter.'

CHAPTER TEN

'This is the most long-winded, luke-warm, lily-livered revenge in the entire history of revenges!' Cat's father fumed. 'You've been sitting at that table for hours, like a mouse scratching at a wainscot.'

'Hush,' said Cat. 'Or he'll smudge the ink and have to start again.'

Me and Lola edged forward invisibly to get a better look. That boy was constantly surprising us. Now it turned out he had a talent for forgery too!

'Why not just run the booby through with a cutlass and have done?' Cat's dad sighed.

Chance sounded exhausted. 'Because I want him to have a taste of his own medicine. And because I am sick and tired of being Nick Ducket's fool.'

Cat's dad shook his head. 'You think too much, boy, that's your trouble. Forget this treacherous knave. Go to sea, get some salt air into your lungs. That's a real life for a man.'

Chance looked startled. 'I'd never considered going to sea.'

'You should,' said the pirate. 'It's a golden time for English seamen. And if you should happen to sink a Spanish galleon or two, you could make yourself filthy rich, and become the master of your own ship like me.'

And then he dropped a total bombshell. 'Cat's coming with me this time, aren't you?' He smiled fondly at his daughter.

Chance blinked. 'I—I didn't know.'

'I'm only thinking about it,' Cat said. 'I haven't decided.'

'She *has* decided,' her dad said calmly. 'I know my daughter and the sea is in her blood. Who knows, you might take to it too. You make a handsome couple, to my mind,' he added slyly.

Chance had finished forging his letter. Now he held the original in the candle flame, watching its edges slowly blacken and crumble. His eyes grew dreamy.

'Maybe I could do it,' he murmured. 'Maybe I could leave England and start a new life.'

His face hardened. 'I can't think about that now. I have a letter to deliver to Greenwich. But this time I'll do it in broad daylight.'

'I'm coming with you,' said Cat at once.

He shook his head. 'No, I've got to go alone.'

Lola smiled mischievously at me and hummed a bar of Reuben's little tune. I knew what she was saying. *You're not alone, Chance. Not now. Not ever.*

*   *   *

Chance had explained his plan to Cat and her pirate dad, which of course meant that me and Lola were also in the know. It was simple but stunningly brilliant.

The old letter named Chance as a conspirator. The new one, also signed by 'Don Rodriguez', named Nick instead, stating that Chance was an innocent pawn, who had no idea what he'd got himself into.

But he was still taking a terrible risk.

It was still possible Chance might not be believed. Which meant he'd be arrested for conspiracy and probably hung, drawn and quartered. Like Michael said, the Tudors were into revenge in a big way. Merely *hanging* criminals was far too tame for them. They preferred to split their wrong-doers down the middle and expose their internal organs as well.

Poor Chance looked so scared as the ferryman rowed us upriver to Greenwich, I truly thought he might be sick. I didn't feel too good myself.

At least this time we didn't have to snake through the trees like commandos. Chance walked right up to the palace guards, where he stood peering anxiously from face to face, as if he didn't know which one of these poker-faced heavies to address. He really was a brilliant actor.

'Excuse me, sirs,' he said in a timid little voice. 'Don Rodriguez gave me a purse of gold to deliver this letter to a lady at the queen's court. At first I wanted his gold, but now I'm scared I might be doing wrong. What if he's plotting to harm our queen? Should we open the letter, do you think?'

As it turned out, that was the easiest part.

The hardest part was when they made Chance take them to Nick's lodgings, then having to watch as they marched his ex-best friend away to the Tower, and hearing their boots tramp away over the cobbles. 'I fear your recklessness will kill you,' Cat had said. And she was right.

I'll never forget Nick's face when he realised Chance had turned the tables. He crumpled like a little kid.

'I thought you were my friend,' he said. 'And all the time you hated me.'

Chance's voice shook. 'I never hated you. But when I was with you, I sometimes hated myself.'

'And now I'm condemned to a traitor's death,' Nick said bitterly. 'How do you feel now, old friend?'

Chance's eyes filled with sorrow. 'Very sad.' He hesitated. 'But also free.'

On the way back in the ferry, he dozed, totally exhausted. I was knackered too. All the emotion of the past few hours had totally drained my angel strength.

And suddenly Brice was there in skintight jeans and a T-shirt.

Sharing a small boat with a furious PODS agent is not an experience I'd wish on anyone. But I kept my voice steady.

'I guess this is goodbye. Since you've dropped the Elizabethan disguise, you must be heading back to Slime City or wherever you lot hang out.'

His anger came pulsing at me in shock waves. 'Don't try to kid yourself you've made a difference, sweetheart,' he sneered. 'You haven't changed a thing. The Agency must be insane giving this mission to a bunch of angel brats.'

'That's your opinion. Thanks to us, Chance won't die a traitor's death. Now he and Cat can go off together and start a new life. Game over.'

His lips twisted into a cold smile. 'Melanie, please! You should get a job writing daytime soaps! You really think I went to all this trouble to thwart true love? You're even more clueless

143

than I thought.'

But I was looking at Brice's face, borrowed from that beautiful boy I'd fancied in the days when I was just another airhead with attitude—in the days before I died and got a life. And it occurred to me that Brice was wrong. I had changed something. Me.

'Brice,' I said. 'How come the Opposition sent you here, when this is a no-go zone for agents?' He laughed. 'They didn't.'

I was bewildered. 'Then who . . .? I mean, who else *is* there?'

'Oh, the Opposition like to call me in when anything interesting comes along. This little project for example,' he added with one of his chilling smiles. 'But I prefer to work alone.'

I felt my skin starting to creep. Suddenly the cosmos seemed weirder and scarier than I had ever imagined.

'Then what *are* you?' I almost whispered the words.

Brice stood up in the boat so that he was grinning down at me, and delivered his best-ever exit line.

'Oh, didn't you know, Melanie? I'm

an angel. I'm an angel, just like you.'

And like a vampire in a bad movie, he vanished into thin air.

* * *

'A fallen angel?' I said to Lola that night. 'So did Brice like, go to our school and hang out at Guru?' I shuddered. The idea was too deeply disturbing for words.

Lola shook her head. 'I think the last time the Agency made that kind of mistake, it was when angels still wore long white robes. And fought with swords,' she added comfortingly.

'All the same.'

We were in Cat's bare little attic. Cat was sorting through her few possessions. Chance was flicking through a book of Elizabethan travellers' tales, occasionally reading the more bizarre excerpts out loud.

It was a sweet scene, but somehow I wasn't convinced.

'Lollie, this is our second shot at a happy ending,' I said anxiously. 'And I'm scared we're going to blow it.'

145

'But this is so perfect,' Lola assured me. 'Chance and Cat are going to have a new life in a new world.'

'But Brice seemed so sure this wasn't a love thing, and he had no reason to lie. We're missing something. Something he thinks I'm too bimbo-ish to see.'

Chance gave an amazed chuckle. 'Cat, according to this fellow, there is one island where all the people have only one foot each! One very *large* foot. He says they move around surprisingly quickly!'

If only Orlando was here to give us some advice, I thought wistfully. Even a passing Earth angel would do.

But for cosmic reasons which I totally didn't understand, me and Lola were the only angels available.

I sighed. 'Lola, we had doubts before and we were right. This time we've got to try to help Chance do the right thing.'

'I know,' Lola admitted. 'I feel the same way.'

'But how? We can't materialise.' I pulled a face. 'And I don't think I really ought to whack anyone again!'

146

'There's only one thing we can do. We totally bomb them with vibes. And trust them to find their true destinies,' my soul-mate added poetically.

I puffed out my cheeks. 'Lollie, I'm trusting so hard, my trust muscles are like old knicker elastic.'

So we did what Lola said. We bombed Cat's little attic until the air felt like tingly champagne.

After half an hour or so, Cat suddenly found her old shell necklace at the back of a drawer. She sat back on her heels, looking wistful.

'My mother gave me this,' she said. 'It's all I have of her. What a wild little girl I was. I loved the sea even then.'

She darted a troubled look at Chance. 'But you get seasick just watching the ships bob up and down in the dock.'

He looked startled. 'I'll soon get used to it.'

'But your job at the theatre—' she began.

'I'm a dogsbody, fetching and carrying, that's all I do.'

'But one day you'll be an actor! It's

what you wanted! Why throw it all away?'

Chance shut his book with a snap. 'Pretending to be someone else,' he said with contempt. 'What life is that for a man? No, Cat, there is no future for me here.' He looked anxious. 'Don't you want me to come?'

'Of course, but—'

'Because you are my life, Catherine,' he said passionately. 'When I wake you are the first thing I think of.'

Lola and I hastily looked away. Eavesdropping is one thing, spying on couples kissing is something else.

'Keep going,' I hissed. 'We've got to keep going.'

And we went on beaming angelic vibes at them until gold sparkles fell like rain.

Cat went on sifting through her things. A comb, a brush, a hand mirror, a lumpy-looking sampler she'd been forced to sew when she was a little girl, some scuffed leather boots.

Then she sat fiddling with her necklace again, and I realised she'd made up her mind to tell her

148

sweetheart some painful home truths.

'Chance, you say acting is no life for a man, yet that's exactly what you've been doing ever since we met.'

He looked stricken. 'Don't say that. I never pretended with you, not when it mattered.'

'No,' she agreed softly. 'Not with me, that's true.'

'With some people, with Nick, it seemed to make things simpler. With you it's the opposite. You're the star I steer by, my compass! Together, we can start again. We can be whoever we want to be.'

She stroked his hair. 'I don't want to be someone else,' she said quietly. 'I want to be me. You're always starting again. You have no roots, no past, Chance. I know absolutely nothing about you. It's time for you to stop running away from everything and stay put for a change.'

I felt a tiny twinge of recognition. I hate to admit it, but I used to be a total escape artist. Then I died and finally found something I wanted to do. But Cat was right. Chance was still all over the place.

'It's all right for you to run away,' he said angrily. 'But not for me, is that right?'

'I'm not running away. I'm following my dream. You must follow yours.'

He buried his face in his hands. 'Cat, you don't know what it's like! There's all these different characters inside me. All these voices. How can I tell which is me?'

Her eyes filled with tears. 'You are a wonderful person, Chance, and it truly breaks my heart to—to—'

Lola and me were trying hard not to cry.

'Will it make a difference if I tell you about my past?' Chance said eagerly. And all at once he was talking at top speed.

'My father was a glover and my brothers followed his trade, curing the skins, and turning them into gloves. Great troughs of animal skins soaking in salted water. They stank the house out.'

The air was electric. Cat was utterly still and Lola and me hardly dared to breathe.

'A few months before I left home, my father's business began to fail. We never really got on. I disappointed him. He said I'd never amount to anything.'

Chance's breath was coming in gasps. It was like, now he'd started to open up, he totally couldn't stop.

'Then my little sister died, her name was Ann. She was eight years old. She had five freckles on the bridge of her nose and she died.'

'Shsh,' Cat said, putting her finger to his lips. 'Don't.'

But he kept talking desperately. 'Money was short. We could barely afford to put food on the table, I went poaching the local squire's deer, and got caught. If I'd stayed I'd have brought shame on my family, so I ran away to London. I thought I'd find my fortune. Then I could go home again, only this time I'd make my father proud of me. But instead I found you, Cat, and you are my home, my heart and now I'll lose you . . .'

Lola and I exchanged agonized looks. And without a word, we softly tiptoed out and left them alone.

*   *   *

I totally couldn't understand Chance. Barely an hour before he was due to see Cat off, he was at the playhouse, scribbling furiously in a notebook.

Suddenly he ripped out the page. 'Eyes full of fire. Hair like black wire,' he said contemptuously. 'An ape could do better.' And he scrumpled up the paper and tossed it disgustedly into a corner.

He only just made it in the end, arriving at the docks as Cat's father was about to help her down into the dinghy which was to row them out to her father's ship.

Cat gave a little cry of anguish and ran to Chance, pressing something into his hand. 'My shell necklace,' she said. 'It's the most precious thing I own.'

'I tried to write you a poem,' he said into her hair. 'But I tore it up.'

They clung to each other, but Cat's father gently detached her and helped her down into the boat.

152

Lola's eyes were red from crying. 'I don't care if it's unprofessional. I can't stand to see Cat so miserable,' she snivelled. 'Some happy ending this is.'

The boatman pulled on his oars and the dinghy began to move away from the jetty.

If he reached out now, he could still touch her, I thought. It was like I totally didn't want to believe it was over. But Chance didn't move.

Then I heard him draw a sharp breath. 'I do have a farewell gift,' he shouted suddenly. 'My name! I want to tell you my name!'

But the wind snatched his words away and the water was widening between them and Cat couldn't hear.

In his desperation, he jumped on to a barrel. 'Can you hear me, Catherine Darcy? I want to tell you my name!'

People were staring. Was this boy out of his mind?

Chance flung out his arms, the wind whipping at his hair and doublet.

'My name is Will Shakespeare!' he yelled. 'I am Will Shakespeare and I love you. I'll love you till I die!'

My mouth totally fell open.

Chance was laughing and crying. Something huge had happened to him. He'd said his real name aloud. He'd lost his one true love. He looked trembly and new, like something which had just emerged from a chrysalis.

His eyes! I thought. All of him is there behind his eyes!

OK, it's just possible I started something that rainy night, with my slightly unprofessional cosmic whack. But the important thing is that Chance finished it. He woke up all by himself, exactly like he was supposed to.

But right now the poor boy was in such a state, he didn't know what he was doing.

He jumped down from the barrel and stumbled away. And before I knew what was happening, he'd walked right through me, like some sort of angel car wash. Then suddenly he stopped, looking around in bewilderment, almost as if he knew I was there.

I was in total bits. Every atom in my body was fizzing with the delicious shock of mingling molecules with the greatest writer who ever lived.

And at that moment, some invisible gate between Heaven and Earth was unlocked, and there was a great whoosh of light.

People actually looked up in awe. They couldn't see what was happening. But they could feel it. It was like an invisible wedding, it was like the May day celebrations, only a billion times better.

All over the city of London, the angels were coming back.

CHAPTER ELEVEN

Days later, Lola and I were in our school library. No, really!

It's actually my favourite building on the campus. It's a bit like a lighthouse, but made from truly magical glass which gives the effect of clouds floating across the outer walls.

Inside it's even better. The ceiling is actually a planetarium. You can look up from your studies and see all the stars and planets doing their awesome cosmic thing.

Reuben was meant to be joining us later. Something had come up at his dojo, so we'd bagged him a seat. The comfy ones on the top floor are in big demand.

Anyway, there we were curled up with a huge stack of books. Lola had her cute spectacles on and looked v. intellectual.

All this book-wormery wasn't entirely our idea. The Agency had asked us to write a report, and we thought we should have at least some idea what we were talking about.

'I can't believe we missed all those signs,' I told Lola. 'I mean, it was staring us in the face. Like the way Chance really perked up when he was writing those love letters, or spinning some incredible yarn. He actually persuaded those crooks that Cat was an elf princess! He wasn't a liar. He was a storyteller galloping out of a control. He was . . .'

'He was a poet who didn't know it,' Lola finished with a grin. She took off her specs and rubbed her nose. 'Hey, wasn't Sweetpea hilarious about that scar!'

Thanks to the brilliant staff at the Sanctuary, Reuben was almost back to normal and his injuries were healing fast. A bit *too* fast for Reuben. He'd actually asked if he could keep one particular scar on his chest. It's shaped like a starburst and is quite stylish in a bizarre sort of way. 'Battle scars,' he'd explained. 'So everyone knows I'm hard.'

'You *are* hard,' I told him. 'You were

a total hero. You fought for your life, even though you were really ill.' Reuben's strange symptoms had turned out to be the effects of severe angelic shock. Human violence really takes it out of pure angels at first. The bear business must have been the final straw.

'That's why I want the scar, Mel,' he'd said fiercely. 'To remind me. I'm never letting some PODS creep up on me again.'

I leaned back in my chair with a deep sigh, and gazed up at the library ceiling, where the planets were doing their stately glittery dance. 'Boys are so weird,' I sighed.

'Hey,' said Lola. 'We've still got work to do, remember?'

We were gradually piecing things together. For instance we now knew that the no-go zone was all the Opposition's idea. Chance was an important Agency project which they were determined to sabotage. This may surprise you, but the PODS Agency has to abide by cosmic laws just like we do. So their lawyers went through the law books with a fine toothcomb, to find something they could use to their advantage.

Finally they found some totally forgotten statute, saying that in the unlikely situation that Earth's light levels ever reached 50/50, all cosmic personnel should be withdrawn, to let the levels settle naturally.

This law was originally intended as a safeguard for Earth. But one of the three 50/50s ever seen in the cosmos, just happened to coincide (yeah, right) with the particular years Chance was at his lowest ebb. In the books, these are referred to as 'Shakespeare's Lost Years'.

The Opposition made it look as if they'd totally tied their own hands, by agreeing with the Agency that they'd only try to influence Chance from a distance. But as soon as the Agency was out of the picture, the Opposition instantly hired Brice to do their dirty work for them. Cosmic laws don't mean a thing to him, apparently. He's the original cosmic outlaw.

Lola was frowning at her notes. 'I

hate to seem thick, but what's the big deal about Shakespeare exactly? I mean, how come both agencies were fighting over his soul?'

'I asked Michael about that,' I said. 'He said the Opposition does everything in its power to make humans forget who they are and what they came to do. But Chance, erm, Shakespeare, actually remembered, and Michael says it shows in every line he wrote.'

Lola looked awed. 'Boy,' she said. 'That was some thump you gave him, Mel.'

'You know what's weird?' I said. 'I've been flipping through his plays since we got back, and I keep seeing all this stuff Nick said. Remember that crack about "Exit pursued by a bear"? That's in *The Winter's Tale*. And that line about a rose smelling sweet by any other name—that's *Romeo and Juliet*. As for Romeo, he is pure Nick! Before he fell for Juliet, he had a different girlfriend every day of the week.'

Lola looked slightly sad. 'I thought exactly the same thing. He's like the sweet Nick, before he listened to Brice and forgot who he really was.'

I suddenly realised I was fiddling with my hair, something I do when I'm upset. 'Tell you what,' I admitted. 'I'm really disappointed with Chance.'

'I know what you mean,' sighed Lola. 'All that stuff about "you are my guiding star and I'll love you till I die".'

'Yeah, then he writes a whole bunch of plays which totally wouldn't exist if it wasn't for his childhood sweetheart, and doesn't give her so much as a tiny mention. Huh!'

'Hmmn,' said Lola. 'He's an Elizabethan love-rat, definitely.'

Someone coughed.

I looked up and turned bright scarlet.

Orlando was standing like, two inches from my chair. He must have heard every word we'd just said.

Did I mention that Orlando looks like one of those dark-eyed angels in an old Italian painting? Did I also mention that he's a total genius? Well, he is. And in two minutes he totally set us straight.

161

'So what did Shakespeare's childhood sweetheart look like?' Orlando seemed genuinely interested. Actually, he seemed slightly excited, and he is usually Mister Calm and Collected, believe me.

So I described Cat's green eyes and golden skin and her springy dark fuse-wire hair and suddenly Orlando broke into this big grin.

'Congratulations,' he said. 'You just solved the mystery of the dark lady.' And he whipped a book off the shelves, *Shakespeare's Sonnets.*

Apparently Shakespeare wrote these poems which constantly refer to a beautiful dark lady, but no-one could ever figure out who she was. It's been driving scholars crazy for centuries!

Orlando gave me one of his heart-melting smiles. 'I think you owe Chance an apology,' he said. 'He didn't forget her. He remembered Cat for ever, just like he promised he would.'

And suddenly there was this embarrassing silence, which I knew I should fill with something intelligent, only I just went incredibly shy and tongue-tied instead.

Then I heard scuffly little footsteps and a muffled giggle. A small bossy voice said, 'Ssh, Maudie—you're not allowed to talk in the library!'

A bunch of breathless nursery-school angels appeared at the top of the stairs. They beckoned frantically.

'Mel! Mel! Reuben says come outside!'

'Well, go and tell him to come up here,' I grinned.

'No! Because he *can't*,' said the tiniest angel hoarsely.

'Why can't he come, Maudie?'

'You've got to come downstairs and see!' She was practically jumping up and down with excitement.

So me, Lola, and Orlando went dashing round and round the spiral staircase and flew out of the door. Then we stopped dead with pure astonishment.

The library building is surrounded by this big green park and several nursery-school children had been busy picking daisies. Now, with great determination, they were arranging their giant daisy chain around the neck of a puzzled, but not completely unhappy-looking bear. Lola and I peered at him, hardly believing our eyes.

'Sackerson?' we said simultaneously.

Reuben beamed at us. 'He just got here. He looks great, doesn't he? Doesn't he look *great*!'